"LOS ANGELES JUST MIGHT AMOUNT TO SOMETHING AS A CITY . . .

Take my word for it, Slocum, this'll be a good place to make your fortune."

Slocum looked at the judge with a new glimmer of understanding, but there was also a hint of fear. Boyer was obviously not a quitter but a man who pursued what he wanted in a ruthless way. Slocum reminded himself to keep a careful eye on his every step—and his back . . .

OTHER BOOKS BY JAKE LOGAN

RIDE, SLOCUM, RIDE
HANGING JUSTICE
SLOCUM AND THE WIDOW KATE
ACROSS THE RIO GRANDE
THE COMANCHE'S WOMAN
SLOCUM'S GOLD
BLOODY TRAIL TO TEXAS
NORTH TO DAKOTA
SLOCUM'S WOMAN
WHITE HELL
RIDE FOR REVENGE
OUTLAW BLOOD
MONTANA SHOWDOWN
SEE TEXAS AND DIE
IRON MUSTANG
SHOTGUNS FROM HELL
SLOCUM'S BLOOD
SLOCUM'S FIRE
SLOCUM'S REVENGE
SLOCUM'S HELL
SLOCUM'S GRAVE
DEAD MAN'S HAND
FIGHTING VENGEANCE
SLOCUM'S SLAUGHTER
ROUGHRIDER
SLOCUM'S RAGE
HELLFIRE
SLOCUM'S CODE
SLOCUM'S FLAG
SLOCUM'S RAID
SLOCUM'S RUN
BLAZING GUNS
SLOCUM'S GAMBLE
SLOCUM'S DEBT
SLOCUM AND THE MAD MAJOR
THE NECKTIE PARTY
THE CANYON BUNCH
SWAMP FOXES
LAW COMES TO COLD RAIN
SLOCUM'S DRIVE
JACKSON HOLE TROUBLE
SILVER CITY SHOOTOUT
SLOCUM AND THE LAW
APACHE SUNRISE
SLOCUM'S JUSTICE
NEBRASKA BURNOUT
SLOCUM AND THE CATTLE QUEEN
SLOCUM'S WOMEN
SLOCUM'S COMMAND
SLOCUM GETS EVEN
SLOCUM AND THE LOST DUTCHMAN MINE
HIGH COUNTRY HOLDUP
GUNS OF SOUTH PASS
SLOCUM AND THE HATCHET MEN
BANDIT GOLD
SOUTH OF THE BORDER
DALLAS MADAM
TEXAS SHOWDOWN
SLOCUM IN DEADWOOD
SLOCUM'S WINNING HAND
SLOCUM AND THE GUN-RUNNERS
SLOCUM'S PRIDE
SLOCUM'S CRIME
THE NEVADA SWINDLE

JAKE LOGAN

SLOCUM'S GOOD DEED

BERKLEY BOOKS, NEW YORK

SLOCUM'S GOOD DEED

A Berkley Book/published by arrangement with the author

PRINTING HISTORY
Berkley edition/March 1985

ISBN: 0-425-07784-5

A BERKLEY BOOK® TM 757,375
Berkley Books are published by The Berkley Publishing Group, 200 Madison Avenue, New York, NY 10016.

PRINTED IN THE UNITED STATES OF AMERICA

1

John Slocum looked over his shoulder into the plume of dust that billowed out behind the carriage. It glowed orange and yellow in the burning August sun and it was so thick that Slocum could see no more than ten yards behind. Nor was the view much better to either side. Slocum frowned at the steep walls of the arroyo closing in ahead, then glanced at the small, sickly-looking man beside him and the heavy tin box between the man's legs. Finally Slocum pulled back on the leather reins wrapped about his wrists and fought the two big greys to a halt. He figured they were about five miles out of Los Angeles.

"What is this?" said the man beside Slocum. "Why did you stop?" He let his right hand drift toward his throat. Slocum guessed he kept a pistol tucked under his coat in a shoulder holster, and that the man didn't trust him very much. The little man's sunken grey eyes were fixed on Slocum's face, suspicious and demanding. "Well?" he said. "Did you see something?"

"That's the point," said Slocum. "How could I?"

"Then let's get moving, man. We're wasting time."

Slocum didn't answer for a moment. The dust cloud they'd raised was dissipating in the still air, and he could feel some of it settling on his face, down his neck, and over his bare arms. It was settling into the sweat already there and it wasn't helping Slocum's mood any more than the nervous bleating of the unhealthy-looking specimen beside him. The restless horses were stepping out a little and Slocum yanked back on the reins harder than he needed to. Then he turned around to study the terrain behind them through the remaining haze. After a moment he nodded toward the rear and said, "Take a look, Judge."

Judge Marcus "Lucky" Boyer swivelled his frail body and followed Slocum's gaze. "Jesus," he said, "do the bastards never stop coming?"

"When it comes to a pile of money," said Slocum, "someone will always be wanting to take it away."

"The scum!"

For a moment they were silent, watching the trail of dust that appeared above the wall of the arroyo beyond the last of its many twists and turns.

"Of course," said Slocum, "some targets seem more tempting than others, Mr. Boyer. I was hearing about your little tin box even before you hired me."

"I'm not surprised."

"Then why do you carry it?"

"Because that's how I prefer to transport my belongings," Boyer said coldly. "Do you have any other questions about my personal business?"

Slocum knew he was supposed to back off, but he'd been taking that kind of talk for six days and he was not only tired of it but hot, thirsty, and covered with dust from hair to boots. "Yes," he said. "Exactly what is it you're carrying in that box?"

Judge Boyer tried to draw himself up in indignation, but his clothes masked the effort. It was clear that the suit had been tailored for the man, but Slocum had the feeling that all his clothes would look too big for him, no matter what he wore.

"That is none of your business," said the judge.

"That's what you think, Boyer. Suppose someone tells us to hand it over..."

"I will never give up this box."

"Maybe *you* won't. I make my own decisions about what my life is worth."

"But you're my bodyguard," the judge protested.

"That's right. I get paid to make sure nothing happens to you."

"Or my possessions."

"But carrying that box just makes the job harder. I'm sure you're being watched in town . . . and now they're following us north. All because of that goddamn box."

The judge let Slocum finish and then he said, "How much am I paying you, Mr. Slocum?"

"All right," Slocum sighed. "All right, you got me there. You keep paying me that well, and no one will get your box. But I still wish you'd put it in a bank somewhere."

"Which one? The one that's about to go under, or the one that almost did?"

"What about the hotel safe?"

"Never," said Boyer. "I'll never let it out of my sight, or trust it to anyone else to keep for me."

Slocum sighed again and said, "Well, let's see how bad these fellows want it." He turned the carriage off the wagon road toward the spreading limbs of an old cedar tree that looked as though it had been growing there for a hundred years, soaking up a little moisture every time there was a good rain. The raindrops would gather in the San Gabriels to the north, collecting and coalescing and finally rushing down the Arroyo Seco, where the heavy old roots would catch all the water they could and then wait for more while the tree continued to offer cool shade to passing travelers. For Slocum and the judge it offered a degree of protection as well. Slocum pulled the carriage in close, to wait for whatever it was that made the trail of dust. A fly buzzed loud in the silence of the desert. The leather harnesses squeaked when the horses shifted their position. A drop of sweat fell from Slocum's nose and splashed on his wrist.

"The least you could do," said Slocum, "is plan these trips only when they're absolutely necessary."

"It's necessary," snapped Boyer.

"You don't have anything definite to tell the widow, do

you? She already knows the bank is going downhill. That your loan probably won't save it."

"I want to make sure she understands just how bad the situation is, Slocum. I'm not sure she truly understands that she may lose the ranch."

"So that was the price of your loan," said Slocum. "You had a mortgage on her land, too?"

"How could I be sure Will Church's property would cover my losses? It was only fair that my investment be protected."

"Of course," Slocum said dryly.

"Listen," said the judge. "*They* came begging to *me* for the loan. Or at least Will Church did. He was desperate to save his bank. It's not my fault they couldn't. But now it's up to me to make sure they don't try any funny stuff, like selling off their cattle or having an early harvest in the groves."

Three men had appeared around the last bend, riding slowly up the wagon road. Slocum saw one of them point toward the tree as they drew closer, and the three riders turned toward the carriage, ambling closer in a seemingly casual way.

"Think they're just stopping to say hello?" said Boyer.

"Sure. And they keep lookin' around like that just to see if there's anyone else to say hello to." The two men laughed, and Slocum looked at the judge. "Aren't you planning to unlimber your gun?"

The judge looked startled for an instant, then smiled. "I suppose that's why I'm paying you so much. No, as a matter of fact, I'll wait a bit. I always like to have a trump card. If you don't think you can handle the situation, let me know."

Slocum nodded, loosening his jacket and the thong on the Peacemaker in his holster while he studied the three men. They looked like typical hardcases. One sported a bandoleer and a short-barreled Winchester, while another had a drooping mustache and a brace of pistols. The third was a plain-looking man who caught Slocum's eye because of the firm way he held himself as he rode, not slouching like the others. He was older than they were, too, with a shock of reddish-blond hair and intelligent brown eyes that watched Slocum carefully as the three hardcases stopped their horses in front of the carriage.

The one with the bandoleer touched his hat brim and smiled. "Good morning, *señors*. Has the sun become too much for you already?"

"Not at all," said Slocum. "There are just times when I prefer to have it behind me."

The man with the mustache glanced up involuntarily, long enough so that Slocum could have drawn and fired, but the one who seemed to be leading the bunch kept his steady eye on Slocum.

The older bandit with the reddish hair leaned forward in his saddle, studying Slocum intently. "I got a funny feeling," he said. "Would you be John Slocum, by any chance?"

"I would," said Slocum.

"I thought so," said the redhead, turning toward his companions. "We come a long way for nothing, boys. This here's the man who—"

"I do not care," bellowed the leader, bringing his rifle around. "We will take what we came for!"

Slocum was already reaching for his Colt. He'd hoped the redhead's recognition would prevent a battle, but he'd also tagged the other two bandits as headstrong and not very bright. They had their eyes on the judge's tin box and whatever was rumored to be inside it, and they weren't about to turn around and go home or consider any other approach. Up till now they'd always gotten their way with fast guns. They believed no one could stop them.

That was the way it always was, of course, and so the look of dumb surprise on the leader's face when Slocum's bullet caught him in the chest was no surprise at all to Slocum. The big man forgot about bringing his carbine into play and stopped to look at the splotch of blood on his shirt as he slowly toppled from his horse. Slocum had already put two more slugs into the second bandit by that time, the first in his heart and then, when he still tried to lift his revolver to fire, Slocum shot him in his right eye. It was all over in time to hear the echo of the three shots fading down the arroyo—almost literally in the time it might take to blink. The back of the second bandit's head exploded, leaving a fine spray of red blood to mingle with the dust in the air, and it seemed a long time after Slocum's third shot before the two bodies hit the ground.

The redhead had not flinched or moved a single muscle during the fight. He hadn't even lifted his hands away from the saddlehorn as a gesture of peace, a gesture that could have been misinterpreted in the heat of battle. His control saved his life. Now he began to shake his head, still looking at the crumpled bodies of his late partners.

"Those boys thought they were good," he said, turning to Slocum. "Damn it, they *were* good. But they were still in knickers when you was blasting your way out of tight spots with Quantrill." The bandit shook his head again, in a kind of awe. "Damn! I've wanted all my life to see someone like you in action, Slocum. Now I'm not sure these old eyes were fast enough to follow. You gonna take me in?"

"Take you in?" the judge yelled suddenly. "We're going to hang you!"

"No, we're not," said Slocum.

The bandit's eyes went back and forth between Slocum and the judge.

"This man tried to rob us," Boyer yelled. "He would have killed us."

Slocum shook his head. "He changed his mind. He tried to stop it."

"Sure. He got scared," sneered the judge. "But he came out here with the intent of robbing me."

"And then he didn't. It's as simple as that."

"Slocum, I'm ordering you to shoot that man where he stands."

"No."

"That's an order. Kill the bastard."

Slocum turned his eyes on Boyer and studied him as if he were looking at a crazed scorpion. "I'm not a hired killer," he said calmly. "I don't do murder."

"You're in it with them," said the judge. Slocum saw a strange light in the man's grey eyes and realized he was clawing for the gun under his coat. Slocum grabbed Boyer's arm with his left hand and held it still in his powerful grip. The gun in his right hand, covering the bandit, never wavered.

"Let me go!" raged the judge. "I'll kill you for the traitor you are!"

Slocum gripped Boyer's arm even harder, making him wince. "Listen," said Slocum, "this man is worth more to you alive than dead."

The judge stopped struggling. "What's that supposed to mean?"

"He'll be spreading the word, Boyer. He'll be telling the other thieves just what he tried to tell those two, to lay off. He'll tell them about me and say it's not worth the risk. And you and me, we'll have a lot easier time of it."

The judge was calming down. His breathing was a little less ragged as he stared at the bandit. "You will do that, won't you," he said.

"Yes, sir," said the bandit.

"You tell them what happened here. Tell the ones who hired you."

"But no one—"

"Tell them it won't work, you filthy piece of scum. Tell them that if their bank fails I *will* put that mortgage into effect, and there won't be a damn thing they can do about it!"

Keeping an eye on the judge, Slocum motioned with his Colt to get the bandit on his way. The redhead slowly turned his horse and with a final puzzled look over his shoulder he retraced his path back down the arroyo. Slocum found himself envying the bandit, wondering whether he, too, shouldn't be riding away from the crazy little man with the tin box. But then, Slocum hadn't liked most of the men he'd worked for in his life—and the judge was paying him at least twice as much as anyone else ever had. He shrugged and got out of the carriage to gather up the dead bandits' hardware, which he stashed under the seat. It was a little harder job to round up their spooked ponies, but Slocum soft-talked them and after a few minutes he had their reins tied securely to the back of the carriage.

"You still going to the ranch?" he asked as he climbed back in.

"Of course," said the judge, through tight lips. "They'll have to understand they can't stop me this easily."

"You can't really think the widow hired those men," said Slocum. "Or Will Church. Why, that would be—"

"Maybe you're getting soft, Slocum. Maybe you're getting too old for this job."

Slocum laughed out loud. "If I was, you'd be dead right now."

"Well, I still say you should have killed that man. I daresay you haven't always observed such delicacy when it came to killing people."

Slocum shook his head. "Looks like you got the wrong idea about me, judge. At least you do if you think I'm going to kill on your orders."

"That doesn't sound like the talk of a man with six wanted posters behind him. How does it feel to be so unwelcome in so many places, Mr. Slocum?"

Slocum felt a flash of the old fire in his veins, a taste of the temper that once had ruled his fists and his guns. But it was true that age could change the way you looked at things, and if there was a time when no man who said such things could have remained alive, then it was also true that Slocum could now use other weapons. "I guess things haven't always worked out the way I wanted," he admitted with a tired sigh. "As a matter of fact, it's downright embarrassing that I've come so low as to take money from a man like you."

"What!"

"It sure is a good thing for you that you struck it rich up in the Rockies, Boyer. You sure as hell wouldn't have amounted to anything without all that money to grease the way."

The judge's mouth fell open, and Slocum felt a little better.

"No one talks to me like that," the little man spluttered.

"Then I guess we're about even, Boyer. Should we let it go at that?"

"It's *Judge* Boyer to you, Slocum."

Slocum grinned. "I guess that's the least I can do, *Your Honor,* seeing as how you must have had to pay through the nose for a title like that."

"You keep that in mind, Slocum. I can buy titles just like I can buy men."

Slocum didn't bother replying. He was picturing the red-headed bandit on his way back to Los Angeles, free and easy, and he was thinking how good it would feel to put some distance between himself and the judge. In the meantime, every day meant a little more money and a longer time before he would have to work again.

But Slocum was also gritting his teeth, wondering how much longer he could work for the man.

2

Gradually the arroyo became wider and began to level out. The wagon road climbed toward the east rim. At the top, Slocum was startled by the wall of mountains which suddenly seemed so close, towering over the great expanse of desert sloping down from the foothills. Over his shoulder to the southeast he saw a cluster of buildings partially hidden by a haze of dust being raised by a great bustle of activity. Slocum caught the judge's eye and pointed with his chin.

"Pasadena?" he said.

Boyer nodded and laughed. "God only knows why there's a city there. I guess that's an example of what looked good to the Indiana farmers who settled it."

"I wonder who had the land before them."

Boyer shrugged. "Probably some Mex, if you can call it ownership. Those damn governors of theirs were giving away grants like it was a fire sale."

"They were still grants."

Boyer looked impatient. "They couldn't have been worth much, Slocum. Not if the land commission gave most of the grants to real Americans."

Slocum glanced at the judge to see if he was smiling, but Boyer wasn't being ironic. He apparently thought it was perfectly fair for a commission of American citizens to seat itself in San Francisco and demand that the Mexican grant holders journey five hundred miles north to prove their property rights, using an alien language, against any latecoming American that felt like claiming a few acres. This had all begun twenty-seven years before and Slocum knew the judge was right: only a few of the grant holders had managed to hold on to their land. Slocum had seen the others, the losers, by the dozens in dark little Los Angeles saloons, drinking the hours away. It seemed that every time he'd passed through the sleepy little town, he'd heard at least one eloquent and violent complaint against the *yanqui* land stealers.

One of the lucky ones had been Esteban Cabrillo, who lived frugally, ranched wisely, and hated debt. As a result, unlike many of his high-living friends, Esteban Cabrillo had never mortgaged even one of the 26,000 acres he and the American surveyors finally agreed on. But Cabrillo was gone now and his daughter Maria was trying to hold the ranch together in a world where Los Angeles was no longer a sleepy little town but a growing, surging city, transformed by the arrival of two railroads and hundreds of thousands of visitors. Even then, according to what Slocum had been able to gather, she might have succeeded, had it not been for the man she had chosen to marry.

Peter Jameson was a dashing young American, the son of an early Californio—those Americans who came to California when the land still belonged to Mexico. Apparently Jameson had fancied himself a banker, and eventually he formed a partnership with another Californio, a friend of his father's named Will Church. Their Church and Jameson Bank, open for five years in the Temple Block of Los Angeles, was now threatened by a bank scare and rumors of failure. But Jameson himself was dead, the victim of a bad-tempered horse Maria Jameson personally shot two days after her husband's funeral.

That story intrigued Slocum. He wanted very much to meet the woman who would coolly—or was it hotly?—fire a bullet into the head of the horse that had killed her husband. Slocum wanted to see how she would react when Judge Boyer explained that his emergency loan to the bank had apparently failed to restore confidence among its customers, that the bank might still go under, and, if it did, then he would have the rights to her land under a mortgage the widow had signed. Slocum had a feeling that neither the widow nor her son would take the news calmly, and he was looking forward to the fireworks. He tried not to think too much about what it would actually mean to them. He figured they had known the risks and decided to take them with their eyes open.

The road ran along the rim of the arroyo and then into a grove of young orange trees before Slocum and the judge came to the Cabrillo house. It was an old adobe that seemed to hug the desert floor, the stucco on its walls cracked and fallen away in places but the colors blending smoothly into the desert under the hot sun.

Beside the house Slocum saw a large garden where a woman stood with her hand shading her eyes, watching them approach. She stood proudly erect, her breasts thrusting against the filmy white cloth of her blouse. Her coal-black hair was tied under a wide straw hat, but Slocum could easily imagine how it would fall in soft curves to frame her full mouth and large dark eyes.

"That's her." Boyer sighed. "Thank God there's no sign of her son."

Slocum pulled back on the reins long enough to let the judge hop to the ground near the garden. Then he wheeled the carriage around toward an irrigation ditch he noticed behind the house. There he tied the reins to a lemon tree, allowing enough slack to let the horses dip their necks toward the water. He also did the same for the two dead bandits' horses tied to the back of the carriage. Then Slocum followed a smaller side ditch toward the garden, eyeing the muddy water as it flowed past the ends of the mounded rows sprouting full cabbage plants and melons. Something about the rich colors of the plants growing from the pale, barren-looking sand fascinated him. He'd never quite gotten used to irrigation and desert farming, not after growing up in the rich bottom land of Calhoun County, Georgia, with its moist black soil almost hidden by the cover of wildly-growing vegetation.

"Then all is lost?" he heard the widow say. "There's no hope at all?"

"Very little," said the judge. "The money I loaned is nearly gone. Mr. Church is trying to find more, of course, but . . ." Boyer finished with a small shrug of resignation.

"Will Church!" said the widow with some heat. "The man who assured me my land was safe!"

"He took the same risk, Mrs. Jameson. If the bank fails he will lose his own ranch and his buildings in town."

"He truly signed the same paper?"

"He did," said Boyer. "Certainly there was every reason to believe this was only a temporary scare. He was confident the bank could weather the storm, with a little help. And, of course, I needed to protect my loan."

The widow leaned on the long-handled shovel in her hands. "The customers . . . they're still coming to the bank?"

"The lines get longer each day, Mrs. Jameson."

"They take all their money?"

"They close out their accounts completely."

"But why? Why can't they trust the bank?" she asked.

The judge could only shrug once more, and Maria Jameson stared at him for a moment longer before she realized he had no answer. She let her eyes wander sadly over the house and the orange groves in the distance and up to the mountains above her homeland. Slocum found himself not wanting to look at her. A peculiar sensation was crawling along his skin and through his gut. His glance fell to the garden and the little wall of earth that blocked the side ditch at the widow's feet. It forced the precious water off into one of the rows between the garden mounds. Several other rows already held similar troughs of water, trapped by other earthen dams between the rows and the side ditch. As Slocum watched, the widow went to work with her shovel. She dug into the pile of earth that diverted the water, deftly flipping the dirt into the gap between the mounds, trapping the new trough of water just as the others had been, allowing the flow from the ditch to move on about two feet to begin filling the next trough. Slocum noticed the play of the woman's muscles under her blouse. He also saw the sway of her hanging breasts as she worked, and the shine of perspiration on her dark skin. He felt a sudden desire, but it died as soon as the woman stopped working and he could once again see the torment in her eyes. He didn't look away this time, and the strange feeling in his gut returned, even more strongly. It was like something haunting him, but he had no idea what it was.

"This was my father's land," Maria Jameson said softly, "and it was his father's before that, given by the governor in honor of his service."

The judge looked at the ground. "I'm sorry, ma'am, but—"

"I had a bad feeling about signing your paper. I should have listened to it, and not to Will Church."

"I truly hope you're wrong, Mrs. Jameson, but it was the only way to save the bank. We had to try."

The widow focused on Boyer. "The depositors . . . they actually see the money you brought in?"

"It's piled all over the counters, all in gold coin."

"And still they close their accounts?"

Boyer Shrugged helplessly.

"I am told it is not the same elsewhere, Mr. Boyer," she said.

"So it would seem."

"There are no lines at the other banks?"

"Well, just the ones waiting to deposit the money they've taken out of the Church and Jameson bank."

Slocum saw a hard shrewdness in Maria Jameson's eyes. "Can you tell me why that is?" she said. "Why they would trust the other banks, but not ours?"

Slocum was curious about the answer to that one himself, but the judge only lifted his hands and said, "Who can tell?

Sometimes there is no logic, no reason for the things that happen."

Slocum scowled and looked away, noticing a plume of dust visible above the orange groves. "Company's coming," he said, nodding in that direction, and out of years of habit he unlooped the thong that held his Peacemaker in its holster. When he took his eyes off the dust cloud he noticed that the widow was watching his every move.

"So you are the big man with a gun," she said when their eyes met. "You protect the little man with the money."

Slocum winced, more for the judge's sake than his own, and said nothing. He didn't think her question needed an answer. But she had another question for the judge.

"Your loan to the bank was six hundred thousand dollars, is that not right?"

The judge nodded absently, still watching the plume of dust.

"And thus my responsibility is half of that amount?"

Boyer looked sharply at the woman. "Now, wait a minute. The mortgage doesn't specifically say—"

"I am talking about a matter of honor, Mr. Boyer," she interrupted. "If I could return to you three hundred thousand of your loss . . ."

"It would still be only half my loss, Mrs. Jameson."

"But surely Mr. Church's holdings are worth far more than that! He has the Temple block itself, the *rancho* . . . and land prices have doubled, at least."

"But who can say what will happen on the open market?" The judge sounded exasperated. He waved his hands in dismissal. "Besides," he said, "how could you raise three hundred thousand dollars?"

"I already have the offers."

Boyer was suddenly alert. "What offers?"

"The speculators . . . the ones they call the 'escrow Indians' . . . they're making offers everywhere. Sometimes I can't even believe the prices myself."

The judge only stared.

"I've had offers on our land in the Altadena Arroyo," said the widow. "For house lots. My orange groves would bring even more, with their water rights. Mr. Boyer, I can repay my part of the loan within . . . two weeks."

"I don't think it will work," Boyer said coldly.

"Why not?" pleaded Maria Jameson.

"Because there is nothing in the mortgage about repayment in half measures."

"But I beg of you—"

"There is also the matter of releasing my liens so you could sell," he interrupted. "I have to think of my protection."

"I would give you my word. Or a contract, if you wish."

The judge shook his head. "I'm sorry," he said, "I don't think it would work."

"How can you say you are sorry," demanded the widow, "when you refuse to consider my offer?"

Boyer shrugged again, and all three turned to watch the lone rider cantering toward them from the orange groves. Maria Jameson flashed a worried glance at Slocum, her eyes dropping to his gun. "It's my son," she said. "Pio Jameson. Please . . . he is proud, and sometimes foolish." The flaring temper Slocum had seen only a moment ago began to fade, the woman's spirit seeming to shrink before his eyes.

Pio Jameson brought his horse to a skidding stop just in front of the garden and leaped from the saddle. Slocum could see that he was born to ride—and also that he was born with a burning temper. He had flowing black hair like his mother's, but his eyes were a brilliant green. Slocum straightened himself a little, to look more menacing with the hope of keeping the boy in line, and Maria Jameson said quickly, "It's not what you think, son. The judge is only telling us that things still go poorly at the bank."

Pio Jameson looked at Slocum first, sizing him up, and when their eyes met Slocum felt something pass between him and the boy. He was also feeling the same strange things in his gut, as if he'd stood on this ranch before, in the same place but at another time. He shook off the feelings to concentrate on what was happening.

Pio Jameson was concentrating on the judge. "I've already heard the news," he said. "My friends in town say the other banks are doing well, but not so the Church and Jameson."

"That's what I was just explaining to your mother," Boyer said. "Sometimes there's just no way to figure these things."

"And sometimes there is," said the boy. He took a step toward the judge and Slocum moved closer to the two of them while Maria Jameson advanced protectively from her side. The four of them had drown closer together as if making a step in some ancient dance, forming a tighter knot of tension in the sun-baked desert beside the garden. "I wonder if it is truly an accident," Pio Jameson continued. "Especially when we have so much to lose . . . and you have so much to gain."

"If you're accusing me of something . . ." the judge began.

"Yes?" said Pio Jameson, and Slocum recognized the taunting readiness, almost eagerness, of a man who wanted to fight.

Boyer apparently recognized it, too. "I was trying to help you," he said furiously. "Without me the bank would have gone under weeks ago."

"Sure. And we would still have had our land."

"It was a gamble," the judge admitted. "If you'd won you would still have your land and the bank and I would be the hero. Instead it looks like I've lost my money, and now I have to protect my investment."

"By taking our land," said the boy. "By taking from my mother and me the only thing of any value we have."

"You knew the risks," Boyer said shortly. "Now stop arguing and listen to me. In two or three days I'm coming back with a man who'll keep an eye on things here."

"What do you mean?" said the widow.

"He wants to make sure we don't sell off our cows," sneered her son. "Or perhaps hide them somewhere."

"They may turn out to be *my* cows," snapped Boyer. "That'll all be up to the courts to decide."

"Of course it will, *Judge* Boyer."

"I have to protect myself, damn it!"

"So do we all," Pio Jameson said darkly. He took another step toward the judge and the circle closed even tighter. "Has my mother offered to pay you back?" the boy asked.

"We've been all through that."

"And you refused?"

"It's not practical. I already explained it to your mother."

Pio Jameson turned very still, leaning toward the judge and letting his cold green eyes study the judge's face for a long moment. Then he took a deep breath and slowly straightened his body, settling himself, like a snake that pulls back and sets itself for the strike. Slocum tensed.

"This is not the talk of a fair man," the boy finally said. "I see you, Marcus Boyer. You call yourself a judge, but I see you for what you are and I tell you now, you will never own this land on which we walk."

"We'll see about that!" roared the judge. "I have your mother's signature, and Will Church's. The papers are all legal. The *law* says I have these rights, and by God I won't let anyone stand in my way!" Boyer wheeled and headed for the carriage, his angry stride kicking up clouds of dust. Halfway to the carriage he looked over his shoulder and called for Slocum, who felt as if he were in a trance. He came out of it suddenly, frowning, and backed toward the judge, still troubled by the thing that he couldn't understand. It was like a balled fist in his gut, a hollow ache in his chest.

The judge was already in the carriage when Slocum untied the reins from the little lemon tree by the irrigation ditch. The two men heard Pio Jameson's voice carrying clearly from the garden, unshaken by any hint of fear. "Hear my vow," said the black-haired youngster. "As God is my witness, you will never live to own our land."

Pio Jameson didn't hear the judge's response. It was an ugly whisper, barely audible to Slocum.

"We'll see," hissed the little man. "We'll see who lives . . . and who does not."

3

The morning's confrontation at the Rancho Cabrillo seemed far away that night as Slocum cut into a finely-grilled steak in the dining room of the Hotel Nadeau, still the most elegant hotel in Los Angeles four years after its construction. Slocum and the judge had long since washed away the heavy layers of dust and sweat and notified the Los Angeles County sheriff of the two bodies lying in the Arroyo Seco. Slocum could appreciate having the judge on his side when the sheriff simply took their statements and respectfully said he probably wouldn't need to see them again.

Now the two men sat at a table covered with white linen, and instead of the sun burning overhead there was the soft glow from quietly hissing gas jets placed around the room. A violin played somewhere, blending with the ring of heavy silver on china and the murmur of cheerful conversations. Instead of the black-haired and hot-tempered Maria Jameson there was the blonde Susan Bently, who normally had impish blue eyes and a happy laugh.

Except that tonight she wasn't laughing. Not that Slocum blamed her; she was the mistress of Judge Marcus Boyer.

When Slocum wasn't keeping track of who had come and gone from the dining room, he was watching the way Susan Bently looked at the judge. It was a mixture of sadness, anger, and disgust—mostly disgust, Slocum thought. Or maybe he just thought so because those were his own feelings. Slocum looked at the judge once more, at the way he slumped in his chair, clutching a whiskey glass against his belly and staring blindly at the plate in front of him.

Slocum had lost track of how many times the whiskey glass had been filled and drained. He'd also given up trying to make conversation.

The blonde tried once more. "I walked down to the depot," she said with forced brightness. "I figured I'd make good use of my time while you were off visiting that woman."

Boyer didn't move or speak.

"I've never seen so many people, Marcus! There were three extra sections on the San Francisco train, two from Chicago, and every single car was jammed with people. I wish you'd been there. The people were so excited, it was like they had a fever. They'd jump off the train and right away they'd start looking for the real-estate men—and *they* were everywhere, too. Everyone was pushing and shoving to be first, shouting at the people with them, dragging their bags around." The girl hesitated, glancing down at the long white fingers of her hand. "I kept thinking, Marcus . . . is that what it was like when they had a gold rush? In the old days?"

Slocum sighed. Susan was barely twenty years old and had no memory of her own of the great booms in Montana or the Rockies or even the Black Hills. Slocum had lived through them as a young man—through the "old days"—and that made him realize he was no longer a young man.

Boyer was remembering, too, but he was smiling slightly and there was a wistful look in his eyes. Slocum guessed that Boyer missed the excitement of the hunt, which was one of the reasons a man became a prospector. Sometimes it didn't even matter whether they found any gold; it was the search that counted, the excitement of the quest itself, the anticipation each day that *this* might be the day of the big strike. Marcus Boyer was called "Lucky" because that day had finally come, in a remote canyon on the backside of the Rockies. One of his claims became the site of a thriving hard-rock mine. He'd sold off shares to finance the awesome job of cutting shafts and tunnels and processing the ore, but he also retained a share that he'd cashed out the year before for a figure Slocum could only guess at. Boyer had loaned $600,000 to the Church and Jameson Bank without batting an eye. No one knew how much he had left, or how much of it—if any—he kept in the tin box which was now sitting in the middle of the table on the white linen cloth. But however much it was, it didn't look to be making the man any happier.

"Those days must have been something to see," said Susan. "Marcus . . ."

The judge looked up when the girl hesitated.

"Marcus," she said, "why don't you get in on the land rush? Isn't that what you want? You could find a choice piece of land, stake it out, find the buyers. Wouldn't that be exciting?"

Boyer's smile faded. "What do you think I've been doing, Susan?"

The blonde looked troubled, which was also the way Slocum felt.

"Sure, you took a gamble on the bank thing," she said. "But suppose you let Mrs. Jameson pay you back the way she wants. Then you'd have at least three hundred thousand. Think of all the—"

"I'd rather have the ranch," Boyer said shortly.

"Sure you would, but—"

"But nothing. That was the deal. It was legal."

"That was the deal when you signed the papers. When the land was worth only half of what it's worth now. And when everyone thought the bank would be all right anyway."

"I can't help that, Susan. These real-estate men you keep talking about—they took options when the land was worth even less than that. Do you think they should all volunteer to pay more? Just because a bunch of yahoos from the East are bidding up prices?"

"Well . . ."

"Of course not! That's what speculation is. It's a gamble. If the trains hadn't come through, or hadn't dropped their rates, maybe all those men would have lost their shirts. Don't they deserve some reward for the risk they took?"

"But Mrs. Jameson will lose her ranch. Her son won't have a thing."

"That's not my fault," Boyer said.

"You could help, though. Maybe there's a compromise . . ."

"I'm no philanthropist, Susan. If I was, I sure as hell couldn't afford to give you all the things you want, could I?"

The girl blushed and looked at the top of the table while Boyer knocked back the rest of the whiskey in his glass and landed it with a loud thunk, only partially muffled by the linen. He reached for the bottle beyond his untouched plate and Susan Bently looked across him to Slocum, a childlike sadness in her eyes that touched Slocum's heart. He scowled and looked away in time to see the entrance of a tall, shaggy-looking man who made his way toward their table. Slocum brushed his hand over his mouth and whispered, "Will Church is here, Judge."

"Christ!" Boyer said mournfully. "Just what I need." He tried to sit a little straighter in his chair.

Will Church was nearing sixty and in the way he walked Slocum could see a hint of the proud figure he must have presented at one time. But now his head and shoulders were bowed and his grey eyes were clouded with defeat. The great mane of white hair was ragged and there was a slight tremor in his arms. When they shook hands, his grip felt tentative and uncertain. Church dropped into an empty chair and a waiter appeared immediately to place a shot glass in front of him. The old Californio offered a listless thanks and filled the glass, but then he left it sitting on the table.

"Nothing's changed," he said, staring at the glass. "The clerks have managed to slow it down a bit. Only two hundred and seventeen withdrawals today. But we still lost nearly eighty thousand dollars."

Boyer made a regretful clucking noise with his lips, without looking at Church. Susan asked if there had been any deposits.

Church glanced at the blonde and came close to smiling. "Not a one," he said softly. "We've gone six days without a new account. But it was nice of you to ask."

The blonde gave him a sympathetic look and Church sipped at his whiskey. He made a face, as if it tasted sour, and pushed back his chair. "Just thought I'd let you know," he said, and got to his feet with what seemed to be a great effort. "I'd say another three days, if we're lucky. Maybe only two. Maybe four." The old man shrugged.

Boyer still didn't look up. "Any luck finding another backer?" he asked levelly.

The old man made a sound of disgust. "Far too late for that," he said, looking directly at the judge. "They can see the vultures, I guess. Maybe they can even smell the corpse."

Boyer didn't say anything and after a moment the man left quietly. Susan chanced another look at Slocum. "That's the worst I've ever seen him," she said aloud.

"He's just facing facts," Boyer said harshly. "It's never easy, but he'll get over it."

"Will you?" said the blonde.

"What?"

"Never mind."

Susan concentrated on spooning a little melted sherbet from a crystal goblet, ignoring the judge's glare. After a while he went back to brooding and Slocum finished his meal, wondering if the good pay and high living was worth all the aggravation. He pictured himself out on the desert, roasting a deer steak over a pile of hot coals, feeling the cool evening breeze on his face. He decided he didn't really need the violins and linen and fine silver. They were a nice change, and he could see how people would get used to them, but things were still a lot simpler on the trail. Slocum shifted his feet beneath the table, aware that he was getting restless. He was also aware, however, that each day he could hang on meant a few more dollars in his pocket and more freedom when he finally got around to quitting.

Slocum was brought back to the present by a long sigh from Susan Bently. He followed her gaze back to Boyer, whose eyelids had drooped and whose nerveless fingers had let the contents of the shot glass drain onto his stomach. There was a large dark stain on his vest, just beneath his heart, which made Slocum shudder. Just for an instant it looked like a spreading bloodstain. Slocum shook off the image and glanced at the blonde.

"It's happening earlier every night," she said in a flat tone, still staring at Boyer.

"Uh-huh," said Slocum.

"Kind of sours the evening."

"I admit I've had better times."

The blonde smiled slightly, casting a speculative look in Slocum's direction. "I'll just bet you have," she said. The look continued another moment longer before she nodded toward the judge. "Might as well put him to bed, Mr. Slocum. You get the box."

The girl gathered up her white shawl and her white brocade purse and stood at Boyer's left shoulder while Slocum took his right. Together they walked him through the dining room. Slocum noticed a flush of embarrassment on Susan's cheeks, and he liked her better for it. He also liked the way her heart went out to people who were suffering, but it made him a little bitter that a girl like this should be with a man like Boyer. The bitterness made him give the girl a cold look as the three of them waited for the elevator to come clanking down. He could see that the look hurt her, and he cursed himself. He knew from experience that there are times when life starts to turn sour, when nothing works right, and this was beginning to feel like one of those times. He also knew it was likely to get worse before it got better.

The big metal cage appeared above them, hanging from its swirling steel cables, and Slocum eyed it distrustfully. This was the first elevator he had seen in a public place and even though he was beginning to get used to it, the thing still made him nervous. But when the gates opened a minute later on the fourth floor, Slocum had to admit he was grateful for not having to wrestle Boyer's sagging body up four flights of stairs. The judge was mumbling a little by the time they eased him down on his bed. Slocum slid the tin box under the judge's pillow, then he and the girl eased out through the door and locked it behind them. Slocum turned to go.

"Wait," said Susan.

Slocum turned back, waiting while the girl glanced at the floor.

"It's so early," she finally said. "And I'm lonely. Did you . . . did you have any other particular plans tonight?"

4

Slocum bought the girl a drink in a saloon down the street that featured a stage show, and he enjoyed watching her come to life. She laughed and seemed to forget her troubles. Later they strolled to the plaza, lingering there for a time to watch the other evening strollers and admire the old family adobes that went back at least a hundred years. Horse-drawn trolleys rattled by periodically, following the iron rails in the middle of the street. City workers had been laying down paving stones, and Slocum listened to the change in the sound of the horses' hooves, plodding from the dirt onto the ringing stone. It made him think about the changes he had seen in the West, and he talked about them a little when Susan asked him why he was so quiet. She seemed interested in what he had to say. After a while they walked some more, returning to the Hotel Nadeau well before midnight. Susan had taken Slocum's arm as they walked, and she squeezed it as they paused in front of her door.

"Won't you come in?" she said with a bright smile.

Slocum glanced down the hall toward the judge's suite. "It might be better if . . ."

"You can't be worried about Marcus," teased the blonde. "He's out cold until at least noon tomorrow, and you know it."

"The thing is," said Slocum, "he's the one who pays my wages."

"Is it loyalty?" Susan asked, genuinely surprised. "To *him?*"

"I guess it's more the idea, ma'am. It's how a man should act."

"I wish you'd explain some of that to Marcus," said the blonde, suddenly bitter. "I might as well be all alone, as far as it goes with him."

"I'm sorry," said Slocum, bowing his head and getting ready to turn away. "I truly am."

The blonde flashed her smile again and squeezed his arm. "Well, since you're working for him, the least you can do is come in and give me a hand with this dress." She pulled on Slocum's arm and he allowed himself to be led inside. Susan nudged the door closed and turned her back to him, bringing one shapely arm over her shoulder to hold a mass of golden hair away from her neck. Slocum stared at the ivory shades of her skin and the delicate curves of her throat, knowing he should never have let himself be dragged into the room. He knew what the girl was trying to do, and he knew exactly what would happen. He knew his limits, and he knew the game he was playing with himself when he thought, *well, you've come this far . . .*

"You can see the buttons," said the girl, "can't you?"

"Yes," said Slocum, his voice a little hoarse. He fumbled with the top button and then the next, his fingers beginning to tremble a bit as the dress folded away to reveal the blonde's gently sloping shoulders and the soft flesh of her back. He saw her shoulders rising and falling with each breath, and heard her breathing get deeper and deeper. Slocum opened the final button, in the smooth hollow of her back just above the promising swell beneath her bustle, and let his fingers brush the skin along her spine. She shuddered and arched her back, moaning softly, and just then Slocum caught a fresh whiff of her perfume. He felt dizzy. He brushed the palms of his hands over Susan's shoulders and bent forward to kiss her neck.

The girl turned into Slocum's arms, eyes closed, the loosened dress covering only the lower halves of her full, heavy breasts. Slocum stared at the shadowy curves between them before he bent to kiss Susan's lips. She put her hand behind his head and pulled him closer. Her kiss became more demanding, hungry, as she went to work on the buttons of his shirt. She spread it wide and ran her fingers through the matted black hair on his chest. Slocum slipped the girl's dress to her waist and took one breast in each hand, lifting and squeezing them gently. Susan closed her eyes and shivered with pleasure, her hands dropping to Slocum's trousers. He buried his face between her breasts while she worked frantically to free his throbbing erection. Slocum gasped with relief when it was free, and gasped again when he felt the girl's long, cool fingers stroking him. If her fingers were still cool, her breath was hot in his ear when she suggested they go to bed.

Slocum helped the blonde slip her dress down to her ankles, holding it while she stepped free. Then Susan knelt to pull down Slocum's pants before standing to press the full length of her naked body against his. Together they stumbled toward and into the bed, a tangle of hungry arms and legs, and it was almost automatically that Slocum slipped inside her.

Suddenly Susan went rigid beneath him and seemed to stop breathing, but Slocum understood as soon as he looked at her face. She was savoring the sensation in a stillness of rapture. He pressed his hips down to thrust as deep inside as he could go, and felt the girl's hips begin to writhe in response. He copied her rhythm, sliding slowly in and out in a delicious torture. The girl's hands roved across the hard muscles of his shoulders and back. He bent to kiss her ear and nuzzle her hair. He rubbed his chest against her breasts.

Susan groaned, and there was new hunger in the movement of her hips. Slocum felt a tighter grip on his cock as he moved it in and out. He watched the girl's fluttering eyelids and heard her rasping breath, driving himself into her. Her hips began pumping up to meet his thrusts, driven by a wild and frenzied desire. Slocum struggled to hold back until her eyes glazed over and she began to arch her back beneath him, raking his back with sharp fingernails. With two more thrusts Slocum was bursting inside her.

"Mmmmm," she said, wriggling her hips, and a wide grin spread across her face. They were both heaving for air, staring at each other. It was a moment before either could speak, and then neither of them wanted to. They stroked each other, kissing, tasting, and slowly they rolled onto their sides, arms still wrapped around each other. It seemed a long time before they pulled apart, and Susan let her eyes drift down over Slocum's body. "I bet you could teach me a lot," she murmured.

It was the wrong thing to say. Slocum stiffened and sat up on the bed. "So you can use it on someone like the judge?" he said.

"I didn't mean it that way, John. I'm sorry."

Slocum scowled. "I know."

"It's just that no one's ever treated me the way you do. You know so much about how to make a woman feel good."

"I don't understand why you stay with a man like that," he said bluntly.

"Because men like you don't have two nickels to rub together," Susan snapped. "Or, if you do, it never lasts for long. And then you're gone."

"I guess you're right on that count," Slocum said with a rueful grin. "I guess we're just too busy having a good time."

Susan smiled, too. "Meaning the ones who keep their money forget how?"

"Or else they're just too worried about making more money."

The girl turned suddenly sober. "That's the judge, all right. And it sure looks like he's got a good thing going this time."

"If the bank fails."

"Well . . . yes."

"And the Jamesons will be left without a penny."

Susan searched Slocum's eyes. "If you feel that way, John, why didn't you say something? You hardly said a word all night."

"Because you were doing such a good job. And I don't think anything anyone says is going to help."

"Why not?"

"He's just being backed into a corner, Susan," Slocum said. "He has to defend himself all the time, and that's just making him madder and madder, so he goes farther back into his corner. If there ever was a chance he'd change his mind . . . I think it gets harder for him the more he feels like he's being attacked; he has to defend himself all the more. He's *convincing* himself."

Susan was frowning, running the tips of her fingers through the hair on Slocum's chest. "You have good eyes, mister. So how do you reach a man like Marcus Boyer?"

"I'm not so sure you can."

"But you can't just sit back and watch him ruin people's lives."

"You don't have to watch," Slocum said harshly. He was thinking more of himself than the girl, remembering the peculiar feelings that had haunted him that morning at Rancho Cabrillo.

"I've thought of leaving him," Susan said wistfully. It's not like we're having fun any more. But I'm getting worried about the things he does."

"You think you might be able to change some of them?"

"Maybe not change them, but . . ." The girl turned toward Slocum and pleaded with her eyes. "Maybe we can do something together. At least keep an eye on him?"

"I don't know, Susan." Slocum had been caressing her neck. Now his hand slid down to cover one of the girl's fine, full breasts—or cover it as well as his one hand could. He squeezed it softly, feeling the shift of its weight beneath his palm, feeling the nipple turn suddenly hard. Susan closed her eyes and Slocum kissed her, thinking of what might be in store for him if he said yes. The girl seemed to be reading his mind.

"We'd have more time," she whispered in his ear. "You could teach me all the things you want me to do for you."

The words, and the unselfish desire behind them, brought a rush of blood to Slocum's head—and to something else. He shifted his body to make room for his erection. Susan giggled and took hold of him in her hands.

"Does this mean yes?" said the girl.

"I just don't know," Slocum said with a sigh.

"Why not, John? What's wrong?"

Slocum had expected her to try to punish him by pulling away, but she continued stroking him, and now she kissed his cheek. He scored that as a point in her favor, and felt a sudden surge of affection that made him want her even more.

"It's the job," he finally said. "It's beginning to get under my skin."

Susan giggled again and said, "I thought that was me."

"Well, you, too," Slocum kissed her neck and started to roll her over, with himself on top, but Susan resisted.

"Let me be on top," she whispered, already raising herself to her knees and straddling Slocum's thighs. She held his cock in both hands, rubbing its tip against the wet folds of flesh between her legs. Slocum stared at her hanging breasts until she leaned forward to brush them against his chest. Slocum closed his eyes and let his hands move over her body, never getting enough of the silky smoothness of her skin. Slowly she was lowering herself onto him, letting him slip deeper and deeper, and stroking him the whole time. He opened his eyes just in time to watch himself disappear completely inside her.

5

"What did you mean about the job getting under your skin?" Susan whispered.

She and Slocum were breathing softly again, and the sweat had dried from their skin. It was well after midnight. The hotel was mostly quiet, with only the occasional clip-clop of a horse's hooves outside.

Slocum frowned and stared toward the dark window. "It started this morning, I guess. When we went out to the ranch."

The girl's soft blue eyes looked worried. "Did something go wrong?"

"Not really. It went pretty much like he figured."

"But something made you uneasy."

Slocum nodded.

"What was it, John?"

"I don't know." Slocum frowned uncomfortably.

"Was it a thing in your gut?"

"Well, yeah. It was a strange thing, Susan. Like the whole day had just happened a few hours before and I'd already lived through it all." Slocum shook his head. "It was like hearing an echo, except I never heard what it was that caused the echo. Does that make any sense?"

The girl nodded. "It happens sometimes."

"But why? I mean, it was like I knew exactly what that boy was going to say to the judge . . ."

Slocum stopped, and Susan shrank from the faraway look in his eyes. But Slocum still held one of her thin wrists in his hand, and now his grip began to hurt.

"John," said the girl, "what's happening? Did you figure it out?"

"Christ," said Slocum.

"John. My arm."

"That boy is me, Susan. It's twenty years ago, and I'm—"

"You're hurting my arm, John!"

Slocum looked at the blonde, only half-seeing, but he released her wrist before he looked away. The girl saw a haunted look in his eyes, and understood that he simply forgot to apologize. She waited for him to speak.

"Christ," he said again. "The years sure change things."

"What things?"

Slocum shook his head. "I *have* been here before . . . except that now I'm the man I killed."

"You're the what?"

"I'm the henchman. And that boy is me."

"You mean he looks like you?"

"No, no. Well, a little, I guess. But I'm talking about the situation. The ranch, the judge . . ." Slocum frowned, and again he had a haunted look.

Susan instinctively touched his face as if to heal whatever was tormenting him. Her touch at least brought him back to the present and he looked at her, realizing that she didn't understand. "It goes back more than twenty years," he said. "I bet . . . When were you born, Susan?"

"In Sixty-seven."

"Good Lord, you weren't even born yet!" Slocum began drifting into another reverie and the girl watched him for a while.

"What happened?" she finally asked.

"Well, there was a judge in the new government . . . after the war."

"Is that what they called the carpetbaggers?"

Slocum nodded. "The judge came one day to tell me that my folks had stopped paying taxes on our farm."

"Where was that?"

"Calhoun County, Georgia. It was my daddy's place, and his daddy's before him. Just like the Jameson place."

"Was it true, what the judge said?"

"In a way. My folks couldn't have paid the taxes too well, because they were both dead."

"I'm sorry, John."

"It was a long time ago. Anyway, I'd paid the taxes as soon as I got back. The judge was lying through his teeth."

"Didn't you show him the records? Couldn't you prove it?"

Slocum opened his mouth to tell her about the way it was, that a man who'd ridden with Quantrill wasn't about to get much cooperation from the Yankee laws and courts. Instead he stared at the window for a long moment, his mouth still open, before he spoke. "I was about to tell you how hopeless it was," he said, "and that the only thing I could do was kill the judge . . . which I did. But maybe that's just the way I looked at it at the time, twenty years ago, as a hot-blooded youngster. I guess things look a little different to an old man." Slocum grinned suddenly. "And to smart young ladies."

Susan smiled, too, a nice shy smile. "Of course, I have no way of knowing what it was like back then. But don't give me that nonsense about you being old." She looked down the length of his body. "In fact, you're more man than I've ever had."

Slocum appreciated the compliment, but not exactly the way it was worded. A shadow flickered over his eyes. The girl misunderstood its meaning.

"Did you lose the farm?" she asked.

"Sure," said Slocum. "Killing a federal judge, not to mention the hired gun he had along with him, kind of seals your fate."

There was a look of dawning recognition in the girl's eyes. "That's a little like what you're doing for the judge," she said. "Is that what you meant when you said you were the man you killed?"

"Life sure is a bundle of tricks, ain't it?" Slocum laughed. "Here I am protecting a man who's more or less trying to do to someone else what I killed a man for trying to do to me. *I'm* the villain of the piece, Susan! I was the villain twenty years ago and here I am on the other side and I'm still the villain. Sometimes you just can't win. Now young Pio Jameson says he'll see me and the judge dead before he lets the judge take his land."

"You mustn't let that happen, John."

"Well, I'm truly touched that you don't want the boy to gun us down."

Susan put her hand over Slocum's mouth, giggling. "You know I don't mean that. If you were too fast for a hired gun back then, I'm not too worried about you now after you've managed to stay alive for twenty years." She turned serious. "But you can't allow a showdown. You can't quit this job. Either the boy will get himself killed, which will leave his mother in a worse fix than ever, or else he'll . . . Tell me, John, what was your life like after you killed the judge and his hired gun?"

Slocum looked so weary and sad for a moment that Susan began to regret asking the question. "You're right," he said. "My life didn't turn out anything like the way I wanted it. I could have built something on that place. I wanted to. I could have had children of my own and passed it on to them. I could have left something *good* behind."

"Maybe you still can, John."

Slocum looked at the girl, to see if their thoughts were the same, and he nodded. "Yeah," he said. "Maybe I can keep that hot-headed youngster from making my mistake all over again."

The girl smiled and squeezed his hand, but Slocum was thinking about himself twenty years ago, remembering how it was to be so young and so sure of himself. He sighed deeply. "Just maybe," he said.

6

Slocum woke up in Susan's bed shortly after dawn and watched her sleeping for a few minutes, thinking of Maria Jameson and her son Pio and the unfortunate turn of events that had brought them all together. He was also remembering bits and pieces of the previous day's conversations, many of which revolved around the Church and Jameson Bank, which was still losing money while its rivals in Los Angeles had begun to stabilize. It was obvious that the widow and her son had suspicions. And now, as he lay beside the sleeping Susan Bently, Slocum began to entertain some of those suspicions himself. Quietly he slipped from beneath the covers, catching a glimpse of the girl's body that made him instantly hard. He tried to ignore his erection as he went around the bed to find his clothes where they still lay on the floor.

In the lobby he scrounged as many back copies of the Los Angeles *Times* as he and the sleepy clerk could find on the tables and chairs, taking them into the dining room to read while he put away a breakfast of steak and eggs. As it turned out, the meal was more satisfying than what he read in the papers. Only a few years old, the *Times* was already considered one of the best newspapers in the area. So far it hadn't done much with the story of the bank scare. Slocum found three stories telling him more or less what he already knew. In the midst of a wild land boom, there had been worries that the banks were making too many loans to buy property at inflated prices. Some local finance leaders wondered aloud what might happen if there was a sudden contraction in prices, causing an interruption in mortgage payments. Would the banks suddenly be holding thousands of acres of over-valued land . . . and very little cash in their vaults? The doubts had sparked a run on the banks, with customers lining up to withdraw their money. All five banks had found sources for quick cash infusions, and the customers had regained their confidence after a few days—except for the customers of the Church and Jameson Bank.

A *Times* article of two days before had reported the news with a kind of puzzled tone Slocum could read between the columns. There were no explanations, just the fact that the lines continued to grow outside the bank building. The story itself wouldn't help matters, of course, but it quoted Will Church and other bank executives as assuring depositors that there was plenty of money on hand to meet every contingency. Church himself had told the reporter that the bank's affairs were in order, and he was confident that the mortgage department was not at all overextended. He didn't sound remotely like the defeated man Slocum had met the night before.

Slocum read all three stories over a second and then a third time, then charged his breakfast to the judge's account and left the hotel after assuring himself that Boyer had not yet made an appearance.

The Church and Jameson Bank was on Spring Street, but Slocum could see the end of a line of people on Fourth, already around the corner before the bank had even opened its doors. As he walked toward the corner Slocum could also hear the pounding of hooves coming up behind him and then the horse's labored breathing. Slocum turned, facing the rays of the early-morning sun, until they were blocked out by the big gelding bearing down on him. The horse ran on by and the rider who had only been a silhouette a moment before turned into a young blond-haired man in work clothes. Slocum watched him pull the horse up short about half a block away and leap down with a great sense of urgency.

He had the wind- and sun-burned skin of a farmer. He threw his reins over a hitching post and hurried over to reach the end of the line ahead of two other men just arriving. Slocum noticed that the farmer, like most of the others in line, was nervously shuffling his feet and peering forward anxiously. Along the line there was the silence of a deathwatch.

Slocum stopped behind the young man he'd just seen arrive, and put a perplexed look on his face. "Excuse me," he said, "this line isn't for the Church and Jameson Bank, is it?"

"You bet," said the young man, glancing only quickly at Slocum and then back at the line itself.

"But why? What's happening here?"

"Haven't you heard, mister?"

"I haven't heard a thing. I've been away for a few weeks," Slocum told him.

"Well, you got back just in time . . . maybe. They say the bank is going under."

"Who says?"

"Everyone! Look at this line. Best get your money out while you can."

"This is terrible," said Slocum. "Is it like this at the other banks?"

The young man shook his head and scowled. "Not any more. Just my luck to put my money where the bastards don't know how to run a bank."

"That's why it's going under?"

"That's the rumor, anyway. They say the bank's been mismanaged, that a lot of money is missing and no one knows where it went."

Slocum looked shocked. "Do you think that could be true?"

The young farmer shrugged. "All I know is I ain't takin' no chances. If I was you I wouldn't either."

"Tell me, where did you hear all this?"

"From the man who has the place up above mine. He come into town on business yesterday, and took his dinner at a restaurant. He heard it from one of the waitresses there."

"Do you know which restaurant?"

The farmer looked puzzled. "Guidice's. But I wouldn't waste my time goin' down there, mister. What if the bank runs out of money while you're gone?"

Slocum looked at the farmer's earnest young face, so dark from the wind and the sun, and found himself thinking again of Maria Jameson as he had seen her in the sun-swept garden by her family home. Her image was sharp in his mind, even after his wild night with Susan Bently.

"I hope you're wrong," Slocum said. "I sure hope you are."

"Was the waitress good-looking?" Susan asked several hours later, in the dining room of the Hotel Nadeau. She was slicing into the juicy white meat of a chicken breast, but she stopped to give Slocum a taunting smile. "First of all, was she blonde or brunette?"

"More like a light brown," said Slocum, a look of mischief in his eyes. "A beautiful soft shade of brown with little golden highlights all through it. She had wonderful big brown eyes, and—"

"I hope she didn't give you anything but information, John Slocum!"

Slocum laughed. "A man can always hope."

"Well, my further hope is that you're not thinking about anyone except me, after last night."

Slocum turned serious, realizing that the girl meant what she said. She was still smiling but there was a light sheen in her eyes, like the mist of tears. "I'll be thinking of you for a long, long time," he said solemnly. But in his mind he again saw the picture of Maria Jameson, and the half-truth he'd just spoken made him a little sad.

"I think you mean it," the girl said softly. "And just for that I'll ignore the fact that you evaded the issue." She finished carving her chicken breast with a delicate grace, and asked Slocum to go on with his story.

"Well, to begin with, this waitress had hair that was

more the color of dishwater than anything, and she was about fifty years old, and I think she was the type that didn't get her fill of giving advice to her children. If she ever had any."

"She sounds sad."

"I think she was," Slocum agreed.

"So she's the one who was spreading the rumors?"

"She said she believed them because she'd heard them from two separate people. I think she was really trying to be helpful, warning everyone who might have money in the bank."

"Who'd she hear the rumors from?" Susan asked.

Slocum shook his head and sighed. "Don't forget I've been at this all morning," he told her. "I don't think you want to hear the name of every single person I talked to."

"It sounds exciting," said the girl.

"Believe me, it was a lot of work. I never knew it could be so much work just talking to people."

"How many?"

"I don't know. Close to a dozen."

"And you finally traced the rumor down to its source?"

Slocum frowned. "Maybe. Or maybe it's just someone like our waitress friend, telling everyone she can. I came up with three different people who'd heard the rumor from the same woman."

"Another woman," Susan pouted. "Who is she?"

Slocum gave the girl a sad-eyed look. "You're not going to like this. She's a prostitute. Her name's Louise and she works in a bordello called the Rialto." Slocum saw a peculiar expression in the girl's eyes. "Do you want to be the one to talk to her?" he asked.

"Oh, no," said Susan. "It isn't that. You're doing just fine. But the name's familiar. I think I've heard the judge speak of the Rialto, or maybe he's talked to someone who works there. I don't remember."

"Then it's a good possibility," said Slocum with some excitement.

"Yes, but, John . . ." Susan reached across the table to

place a thin white hand on his arm. "It could be dangerous."

"That's all right. I never much—"

"John," she said, "please be careful."

Their eyes met and there was a sudden stillness between Slocum and the girl, broken by Marcus Boyer's strident voice over Slocum's shoulder.

"Well, I'm glad to see you two getting acquainted," he said, sitting down at the table. "I suppose it gives you something to do when I'm indisposed."

Susan pulled her hand away as if Slocum's arm was a burning coal, and flushed a deep red. Slocum groaned inwardly. The girl tried to stammer an explanation, but the judge acted as if he didn't hear her. "Believe it or not, I'm ready for a fine luncheon," he said brightly. "Mr. Slocum, how was that steak? Would you recommend it?"

"It was just fine," Slocum said mildly, apparently oblivious to the judge's harsh glare. "If they slice it off the same carcass, you got nothing to worry about."

"I always have something to worry about," Boyer snapped. "As a matter of fact, we have a busy afternoon ahead. We're hiring men to act as overseers, one on the widow's ranch and one on Will Church's place. We'll be taking them out tomorrow."

7

They set out the next morning at six o'clock, Slocum and the judge and two sour-looking men who carried one new Colt and one new Winchester apiece. The judge had supplied the hardware, but Slocum never quite understood how he found the men. Boyer had simply placed a call from the telephone at the hotel desk, insisting that he crank the machine himself and using a low voice to tell the operator who he wanted to talk to. Slocum had watched him wait a minute or so, and then heard him say, "This is Judge Boyer. Send them over." Within an hour or so five men had appeared at the door of Boyer's suite, to be interviewed one by one as Slocum watched impassively, alert for any attempt to rob his employer of the important tin box. Slocum heard each man describe his background and relate some of the tighter scrapes in which he'd found himself. One of the five was obviously a liar, and Slocum thought two more were questionable. The judge's opinion was apparently the same. He dismissed the same three in favor of the remaining two, one of whom had been a Texas Ranger and was given the ax because he tended to treat prisoners too roughly—or so he said. The other one had been a shotgun guard on the gold coach between Cheyenne and the Black Hills. The railroad had finally come to Rapid City the year before, costing the man his job.

To these two men Boyer explained the job he had to offer, the job of keeping an eye on the ranches belonging to Maria Jameson and Will Church. The overseers would accompany the owners or the foreman and make sure that no cattle, machinery, or other valuable property was moved off the land. They would also see that nothing was destroyed, and make sure that none of the land was sold off to unwary buyers. The men accepted the jobs in a grim manner that made Slocum nervous, grateful for work that didn't mean clerking in a store or picking fruit off a tree. To Slocum the two new overseers looked like the kind of men who'd do anything else to keep food in their bellies, legal or illegal. He'd seen thousands of their type across the West, mostly in smoky and foul-smelling saloons. He'd never seen one behind a counter or driving a trolley car or performing any other job of honest work.

In short, Slocum knew the men spelled trouble. And the judge was taking one of them to Rancho Cabrillo, to Maria Jameson.

There had been no chance for further conversation between Slocum and Susan Bently. The judge drank only wine with the evening meal, and watch Slocum and the girl suspiciously as he ate. Slocum had to suppress a smile whenever Boyer would look up suddenly from his plate, hoping to catch a furtive glance between his bodyguard and his mistress. After the first time, when the judge fell to studying his plate too long, Slocum would make a point of staring at some distant object with apparent boredom. Susan had recovered from her earlier mistake and was able to put on a similar show of indifference for the judge. Finally the three of them had fallen into casual conversation, during which the judge proposed that he and Susan go to the theater. That meant Slocum would go along as well, since he must never stray far from the strange little man in full evening dress, carrying a tin box under one arm.

Susan had managed one furtive backward look as Boyer closed the door of his suite behind them at the end of the night. That brief look came back to Slocum throughout the day as he guided the judge's carriage across the desert, first to the Church ranch near the San Gabriel Mission, then north through Pasadena toward Rancho Cabrillo. Slocum had seen the girl's soft blue eyes for only a moment, but in them he had read regret and sadness, perhaps loneliness. The last was the thing that troubled him the most. Slocum believed that Boyer would care little for the girl beyond the prestige and physical pleasure her beauty could bring him—and *that* thought, with its too-bright images of the judge panting between Susan's legs, gnawed painfully into Slocum's mind. But Slocum knew the girl had more to give than Boyer would ever understand, and if that was true then she would feel very alone whenever she was with him. To Slocum that was the worst kind of loneliness. So when he remembered the door closing on the two of them, two things were happening at the same time. Slocum was grateful for that last look, because it took away some of the sting of the pictures forming in his mind. But he was also saddened by everything else the look made him think of. He wondered if Susan would eventually be able to find a life to make her happy.

"These people are all such fools," said Boyer.

"What?" said Slocum. "Who?"

The judge lifted his chin to point out over the barren desert through which they were passing, and Slocum noticed the sidewalks there for the first time that day. He had seen them before, almost everywhere he traveled in southern California, but never in quite so remote a location. They were four miles northwest of Pasadena, and it had been almost that long since they'd seen a house or a store. Yet, leading away from the wagon road, on both sides, boardwalks had been built through the sparse sage and grass. They were meant to be sidewalks, outlining future streets seen in someone's imagination, and all along the sidewalks Slocum could see the surveyors' pickets and colored ribbons outlining available lots for sale. It gave Slocum an eerie feeling to see the sidewalks, as if they were the remains of some long-dead ghost town instead of the hope for a bright future. Even more absurd—something like a mirage—was the sight of a large wagon rolling along between the sidewalks. It was pulled by a team of four and it, too, was brightly decorated with ribbons. Makeshift seats had been rigged in the wagon and they were filled by men and women of all ages and dress, listening to the spiel of a man who stood in the front of the wagon as it rolled along. He held a megaphone to his mouth and some of the phrases came back to the judge's carriage, a little out of kilter with his sweeping gestures.

"Crestview subdivision..." Slocum heard him say. "...back door a view of the majestic San Gabriels...growing city and your chance... more sunshine than you've ever...anything grows in...plan for the future...plenty of financing available."

"Such utter fools," Boyer muttered. "Look at them! They've just stepped off the Santa Fe in Pasadena and right away some "escrow Indian" swoops down on them with a line of horseshit in one hand and easy credit in the other. "Sell the farm in Iowa," he tells 'em. "Get rid of the dry-goods store in Albuquerque." He tells 'em anything grows, but he forgets to mention that you need water and the nearest ditch is four miles away. Those operators are getting title to every swamp and rocky hillside they can get their hands on. And when they get done parcelling out their lots, an acre that might have been worth a hundred dollars is selling for seven or eight thousand."

"If they sell all their lots," Slocum reminded the judge. "And if the customers keep up their payments."

Boyer frowned. "Very good, Slocum. I didn't realize you had a mind for business along with everything else."

"I doubt I do, Judge. I've just been around a long time and seen a lot of booms. You know as well as I do what'll happen. There won't be any houses on that land for another fifty years, and that man with the horn...I give him two years before he's flat broke."

"Some people will make a fortune," the judge said wistfully, "but you're right about most of them, Slocum. A lot of suckers will lose a lot of money, and when the bust comes there'll probably be a couple more busted banks if they don't cover their asses. But one good thing..."

"What could that be?"

"There'll be a lot of people stuck out here who can't afford to go home. They'll have to do something. I would never have believed it a couple of years ago, but Los Angeles just might amount to something as a city. It might even turn out to be the biggest city in southern California."

"A lot of people are betting that'll be San Diego."

"Sure. It's a beautiful harbor. But I don't know." Boyer squinted into the distance. "I just have a *feeling* about this place. The same way I had a feeling about the other side of the Rockies. Take my word for it, Slocum, this'll be a good place to make your fortune."

Slocum looked at the judge, then turned to the quiet man in the back seat. "What do you think, Pierce?"

The man named Pierce, who'd been the guard on the treasure coach, shrugged his powerful shoulders. "I'm not too big on cities," he said indifferently. "I'll be long gone anyway."

"Where to?" said the judge.

"Arizona, maybe Alaska. I'm figuring there's still a little gold in the ground somewhere, with my name on it."

"That's always possible," the judge said slowly. "There's still a little open space left in this country. But you gotta have the nose for it."

"I been doin' nothing but smelling gold for the last four years," said Pierce. "I figure I must of brought a few million down from the hills."

"But don't forget," Boyer said, "most of that gold came out of hard-rock mines like the Homestake. They're not doing much sluicing any more, are they?"

"Just a few hydraulic outfits."

Boyer nodded wisely. "Exactly. You can make a few bucks on a placer claim, but it takes capital if you want to make any kind of real money, boy. Find yourself a quartz claim and then hang onto it with everything you got. Get yourself a lawyer if you have to. But when the syndicates come in, don't sell all your rights. Hear me? Hang onto a percentage, like I did. Let them bring in the equipment and do the digging for you. Then your shares will bring in a nice, steady income as long as you want, and they'll also be worth a hell of a lot of money when you're ready to sell."

"You pay attention," Slocum said with a teasing grin. "The judge is telling you his own success story."

"Damn right!" said Boyer. "If I can do it anyone can, as long as they don't give up."

"How long did it take you?" said Pierce.

Boyer didn't say anything for a moment, and then he sighed. "Too damn long," he said. "I must have been out there twelve years."

"Twelve years!" said Pierce, and Slocum could see that he looked a little green around the gills. "You was prospecting twelve years?"

Boyer nodded. "Yup. But I was a free man, son. Roamed the West and seen things you might never see. I wasn't indoors in some damn store. You hear me good: the ones that quit after a year or two, they're the ones still grubbing for a living. You gotta stick with it, like I did, and you won't ever have to work again, like I won't."

Pierce didn't say anything, but he was frowning at the horizon. Slocum figured he was thinking about how long twelve years could be. Slocum was thinking about the same thing, thinking about the way a man's mind might be warped by twelve years of solitude and disappointment. You could start believing that all of nature was against you. Slocum looked at the judge with a new glimmer of understanding and even sympathy, but there was also a hint of fear. Boyer was obviously not a quitter, but a man who pursued what he wanted in a ruthless way, particularly when he felt attacked. Slocum reminded himself to keep a careful eye on his every step—and his back.

They arrived at Rancho Cabrillo in mid-afternoon, when heat waves shimmered off the sun-baked desert and seemed to engulf the carriage. Slocum felt as if his eyeballs were burning in their sockets, and even the leather reins had stopped feeling cool around his wrists. Maria Jameson and her son had escaped the heat beneath a brush arbor in a corner of the courtyard within their home. It looked like a peaceful setting when Slocum first followed Boyer and Pierce through the heavy beams of a doorframe. But when the widow and her son rose to meet them, the anger in their eyes and the challenging way they stood suddenly made Slocum think of a boxing ring. Except it was more serious than that. Pio Jameson had his gun strapped on, hanging low on his hip in a finely hand-tooled black leather holster. There were silver conchas on the belt for ornamentation, but the holster itself had a well-worn look that went with the way the boy's hand hung loose beside the butt of his revolver. Slocum also saw the way the boy's keen eyes were measuring the three newcomers, watching their placement. Slocum eased off to one side, hoping to flank the boy and keep him from doing anything stupid. But he also started planning another approach should trouble come.

"I'm very sorry to have to make this trip," the judge began. "The situation in town is worse than ever, and I'm afraid I'll have to leave my man here—" he nodded at Pierce. "—to make sure my interests are protected."

"You mean to kill us if we make any trouble," Pio Jameson declared.

"Please,'" said his mother. "Please, my son, do not start anything."

"They are the ones who start it," he said hotly. "We can't lay back and let them walk all over us."

Maria Jameson glanced fearfully at Boyer and Pierce and finally at Slocum, her eyes dropping to his gun as if she couldn't help herself. Slocum caught himself wondering how his life might have been different if his own mother had lived through the War. Would she have been able to keep him from killing the carpetbagger set on stealing Slocum's Stand? John Slocum looked into Pio Jameson's fiery young eyes, saw the hair-triggered temper of his own youth, and knew the answer. He thought about the way his mother might have felt, seeing her son either gunned down or running from the law, and in that moment he shrugged off his memories to concentrate on trying to keep the events of twenty-odd years ago from repeating themselves.

"Now listen to me," Boyer said quietly. "There's no need to be afraid of anything. This is Tom Pierce. He's been a guard on the Deadwood treasure coach for the last four years, and he doesn't mean you any harm. I certainly don't. This is all business, and nothing more."

"To you it's business," said Pio Jameson. "For us it's a question of how to live."

"Life can take some hard turns." said the judge. "We still survive."

Slocum saw a kind of veil come over the boy's eyes and he figured the time was near. He started moving in a little closer. The boy was still talking to the judge. "Tell me," he said, "have you given any more thought to my mother's offer?"

Slocum had eased his way almost to within arm's reach of the widow's son. Some fighter's intuition recognized the tension in the boy's muscles, the alert fixation in his eyes.

"Of course not," said the judge. "It was a foolish notion to begin with."

"Not as foolish as—"

"Don't!" yelled Slocum, stepping forward. "He doesn't have a gun. Your fight is with me."

"But he is the one who steals our land,"

"And I'm the one he's hired to protect his life. That is my job. If I didn't do my job, I would be dishonored."

Slocum figured the boy would understand that kind of talk, and Pio Jameson looked at him respectfully, if nervously. Over his shoulder Slocum saw the fear in the mother's eyes, the alarm in Boyer's eyes. Apparently the judge didn't realize how close he'd come to getting shot at. Tom Pierce was back by the wall, holding a rifle but unsure of himself. For a moment they might all have been statues, frozen in expectation. Finally Slocum squared off in front of the boy, barely two feet away, and said, "Well?"

Pio Jameson licked his lips, looking toward the judge and then into Slocum's face. His own eyes lost their uncertainty, replaced by the same hooded look of concentrated hatred.

Slocum was waiting for more talk, which very nearly lost him control of the situation. Pio Jameson had decided the time for talk was past. Without warning his hand was sweeping up past his holster, grabbing the gun and pulling it free. But even though he was caught unprepared, Slocum's long years of instinct took over. He was reaching for his own gun almost before he knew what he was doing, and it was only the decisions he'd already made, the plans he'd laid out to deal with the boy, that kept Pio Jameson alive. With the barrel of the boy's gun almost levelled into Slocum's gut, Slocum was smashing the barrel of his own gun down onto Pio Jameson's arm. It was almost as much a reflex as his draw had been, but it worked. The boy yelped in pain and dropped his gun, holding his arm against his stomach.

Suddenly Pio Jameson dropped to his knees, scrabbling for the gun with his left hand. Slocum kicked the gun out of his hand. The boy immediately dove into Slocum's knees and Slocum tapped him behind the ear, just hard enough to stun him. Pio Jameson rolled on his side, the stinging fingers of his left hand holding his paralyzed right arm. The boy kept rolling, getting to his knees again and struggling to stand.

"Give it up," Slocum said softly. "You needed a lot more practice, son. You weren't even fast enough that I had to kill you."

"You should have!" Boyer exploded. "All you've done is persuade him he'll have to backshoot us."

"Never," gasped the boy. "You only talk of your own cowardly ways, not the ways of a man."

"Are you sayin' I ain't a man?" Boyer yelled. He was

reaching inside his coat, and Slocum pointed his gun in the judge's direction.

"Leave it be," Slocum said wearily. When the judge refused to stop he added, "If you shoot the boy I'll kill you."

Boyer finally stopped with his revolver just out of its shoulder holster, still half-hidden by his coat. He was staring at Slocum with a surprised look on his face. "You work for me," he said.

"That's right," said Slocum. "Right up till the second you shoot somebody who can't shoot back."

"I'll kill you for this, Slocum."

Slocum shook his head. "Not when you stop and realize I saved you from a bad mistake."

"What mistake?"

"Getting yourself charged with murder, for one. Not to mention what that would do to your chances of using the mortgage without a challenge."

"Then you should have let him kill me," said the boy, still on his knees. "It would show him for the kind of man he is, and my mother would not lose her home."

Maria Jameson dropped to her knees beside her son and threw her arms around his shoulders. "But the *rancho* is for *you*, my son. It would mean nothing without you. I would rather be dead myself."

"Listen to your mother," said Slocum. "She knows what is important and what is not."

Pio Jameson made a sound of disgust. "It is important to have honor," he said, eyeing Slocum scornfully. "If this man steals my home, I am dishonored as long as I remain alive and allow it to happen. This is something you could know nothing about."

Slocum sadly shook his head. "You know nothing about what I know and don't know," he said. "With the years, you learn that there are often many paths that reach the same goal. The paths are all closed if you're dead."

Maria Jameson looked up at Slocum with dark eyes full

of gratitude and depth of feeling. Slocum stared at her for a moment, a powerful feeling of his own stirring in his chest and between his legs. He tore his eyes away from her and looked at the judge, hearing the loud voice inside that told him he was on the wrong side in this fight. Boyer seemed to know it, too. He was watching Slocum with cold, spiteful eyes.

"Shall we go?" said the judge. "That is, if you're done offering advice to these people?"

"Yeah," said Slocum, as if he was thinking about it. "I'm done."

8

The ride back to Los Angeles was a long and quiet one. Judge Boyer was locked in a stone-cold silence for which Slocum would have been grateful except that he knew he should be worried. The judge's silence was a thoughtful one, and every once in a while Slocum felt himself being observed. Boyer had never been much on trusting people. Now Slocum knew his behavior at the ranch had given the judge even more reason to question his bodyguard's loyalties. It was obvious to Slocum that his days with the judge were numbered. At one time he had counted on his superiority to keep the job, knowing that Boyer would be reluctant to fire a man with Slocum's experience and well-honed fighting instincts. But what good are instincts when your man isn't doing the job the way you want it done? When he isn't killing the people you want to have out of your way?

Slocum glanced at the judge, who was staring at Slocum. Their eyes locked in an ancient kind of combat—or perhaps preliminary to combat. They measured each other, tested each other, each man refusing to show any sign of weakness. It was Slocum who finally looked away, to make sure the team wasn't taking the carriage into a ditch. He was relieved to find that it wasn't, and relieved to think that this might be his last ride beside this sour little man. But he was also troubled by the thought of what might happen in his absence. Had anyone but Slocum accompanied Boyer on this day's ride, Maria Jameson would at this moment be weeping in despair, alone and uncomforted, over the cold body of her only son.

Boyer rode to the livery barn with Slocum and together they walked back toward the Hotel Nadeau, the judge holding his tin box conspicuously under one arm while Slocum tried to make his gun equally conspicuous. It was already early evening and the streets were filled with people, but no one seemed to take undue notice of Marcus Boyer. Slocum began to relax as they neared the great sandstone arch that marked the entrance to the hotel.

They were still several yards from the arch when Will Church appeared from the heavy shadow beneath it and began walking toward them. He walked with a steady purpose that made Slocum alert. Later he would realize it was the walk of a man who had already made up his mind to something. Church's eyes were no longer lost and empty-looking, but burning with intensity. Only the slight tremor remained in his arms and legs.

"Hello, Will," Boyer said stiffly. "Are you bringing me some news?"

"Not yet," said Church. "We might be able to hang on another two or three days yet."

"Still no change in the lines?"

"You know better, Marcus." The old man glanced at Slocum and licked his lips, taking a noisy breath before speaking again to the judge. "I've come to ask you to reconsider Mrs. Jameson's offer."

"How do you know about that?"

"I rode out to see her yesterday. Marcus, you must realize how terrible I feel to be taking her down with me. I don't mind so much for myself. I'm an old man, with nothing much to look forward to. But for Maria and her son to lose the ranch . . ."

Boyer was shaking his head. "It's a sad situation, isn't it? But you accepted those risks when you signed the agreements."

"Who could have known that this would really happen?" Church said brokenly. "There was no reason to believe it was anything but a temporary scare."

"Ah, but a good businessman must always prepare himself for the worst possible case. Don't you agree?"

The old man slowly nodded his head. "I never claimed to have a first-rate mind for business," he said, looking into Boyer's eyes. "But sometimes you have to think of other things besides making money. I'm pleading with you, Marcus—begging you—let the widow raise your three hundred thousand. Keep my mortgages for the other half. My ranch alone is worth your investment, and my holdings here in town will probably double it. Isn't that enough to satisfy you?"

The judge sighed and made a show of looking off into the distance, his hands on his hips, and Slocum used the break to think about the warnings his instinct was sounding. He noticed the expectant way Will Church was watching the judge, as if there was a lot riding on the answer he was about to give. It also occurred to Slocum that Church had been waiting for the judge just inside the hotel, to reach him before he went inside. It seemed odd to Slocum that the old man wouldn't try to present his case over a congenial dinner, or relaxed in the overstuffed chairs of the hotel lobby. In light of all those nagging questions, Slocum began to wonder what might be concealed by the loose-fitting buckskin jacket Will Church was wearing. He'd already unlooped the thong from the hammer of his Peacemaker for the walk through town. Now he eased his legs a little farther apart, squatting slightly for a better balance.

"I'm sorry," Boyer finally said. "I truly am, Will. I was trying to think if there was any way I could possibly accommodate you. But you know this boom can't last. It's only a question of when the bubble bursts, and if it happens before I've sold your ranch or the lots in town . . . well, then I'm just out of luck. Values will be down. No one will have any money to buy. The banks will be tight on credit—"

"But you'll have the *land,* Marcus! What a grand thing it will be to have all that productive land, raising crops and bringing in the rents. You certainly can't be hurting for operating cash. You'll have Maria's three hundred thousand—that's enough to set any man up for life—and, for what it's worth, you'll have my undying gratitude, as well as the knowledge of what you've done for those people."

"At great expense to myself, Will."

"How much can one man need? You have more than enough already to make you happy."

"I'm sorry," said the judge.

"What about your reputation in Los Angeles, Marcus? Everyone would love you when they learned what you'd done."

Boyer laughed scornfully. "Who wants their love?" he said. "I'd also be known as the biggest fool on the West Coast."

Slocum watched the old man's last hope slowly dissolve from his face. He seemed to age ten years in as many seconds. "Maria Jameson trusted me," he said bleakly. "I can't bear the thought of her losing everything simply because she trusted me."

"I'm sure you explained the risks." Boyer said. "Even if you minimized them, I'm sure you said enough that she could make an intelligent decision."

Will Church stared at Boyer for a moment, glanced at Slocum with a speculative look, then turned away without a word. Slocum watched him shuffling away, puzzled, beginning to doubt his instincts. He saw the old man run a bony hand through his hair, bringing the hand down along the front of his body. Slocum tensed. When Church's hand reappeared at his side there was a gun in it. Church was turning back toward the judge, facing him from ten feet away. Slocum drew his gun before the old man finished turning around, but he held his fire. Church's gun was still hanging by his side.

"I can't live with it," Church said. "I can't stand to be around when you take that boy's land away from him."

The judge's body had gone rigid. Now he murmured Slocum's name out of the side of his mouth.

"Put the gun away," Slocum said. "I've already got you covered."

Will Church didn't move.

"Slocum," said the judge, a little more urgently.

Slocum began to move closer, hoping to disarm the old man. "Hold it!" Church said. He whipped the gun up and the judge was looking down the barrel.

"Slocum," said the judge.

"Don't do it," pleaded Slocum. He slipped the hammer back on his Colt and kept his eyes focused intently on the uncocked hammer of the old man's gun, and the slack finger around its trigger. He knew he would have to fire at the first sign of movement. "Put the gun away, Mr. Church."

"It's too late for that," Church said, giving Slocum a knowing glance. "Too late for me."

"Slocum!" said the judge.

Church licked his lips and looked at Slocum one more time. Then his gun arm blurred as he raised it toward eye level. Slocum shot him in the heart. Will Church staggered back a step and dropped his gun. It clattered loudly on the boards of the sidewalk in the strange silence that followed Slocum's shot. The old man pulled his jacket aside and bowed his head to look at the blood spreading on his starched white shirt. His head was still bowed when he collapsed to his knees and rolled loosely to his side.

Slocum had slipped his gun into its holster. He knelt beside Will Church and brushed the tousled white hair off his forehead. "You old son of a bitch," he said. "You used me, didn't you?"

The old man's eyes looked at Slocum vaguely. "It's all right," he said softly. "I thank you, sir." His breath rattled and began to fade and at some point Slocum knew the old grey eyes weren't seeing anything any more. He stood up and slowly became aware of the crowd that circled him with its loud buzz of conversation.

He also heard a girl's voice yelling, "Let me through. Let me pass." The voice worked its way closer, and Slocum knew it was Susan's. He scowled darkly at Will Church's body and at the judge, who was standing off against a building with an expression Slocum couldn't read. It might have been shock, it also might have been simple annoyance.

"My God!" Susan said. Slocum turned to find her staring at him across the old man's body. "You killed him, didn't you?"

Slocum nodded dumbly. "I couldn't help it."

"You bastard!" cried the girl.

Slocum opened his mouth to say something, but couldn't figure out how to begin explaining what had happened. As he hesitated, he realized nothing he could say would help. "There was no way to prevent it," he said helplessly. "I tried, Susan."

The girl only stared at him. It came to Slocum that she was probably hoping he could deny it all, but when he couldn't—when he only continued to stand there with his hat in his hand—some spark of life went out of her eyes. Without another word she turned away. The crowd opened before her and then swallowed her up.

Slocum stretched his neck a little, trying to catch sight of her again, but she was gone for good.

9

Darkness had come to Los Angeles and John Slocum was standing beneath an electric street lamp at the corner of Fourth and Spring. His head was thrown back and he was staring up into the light, apparently transfixed by its brilliance. "It sure is a different world," he whispered to himself. "Electricity that's so powerful it can jump through the air . . . and now they're saying it can run a street car. People can talk into a little box and someone else can hear 'em miles away. Elevators in hotels . . . for people!" Slocum slowly shook his head, and suddenly felt the whiskey he'd been drinking. He staggered slightly, cursing himself, then rolled his head back once more to stare into the brilliant arc light.

"Well, here I am," he muttered at the lamp. "Miss Susan Bently—bless her little heart—she thinks I'm a bastard. An' old Will Church didn't feel up to killing himself, so he let me do it for him. Then there's the judge, who didn't trust me worth a damn. And you know what? I think maybe he's right. Susan, too. What do you think?"

The arc light hissed and sputtered in the silence.

"No, I guess you don't got much of an opinion," Slocum said. "You just let us see ourselves the way we really are and let the chips fall where they may." Slocum looked down at himself and the stark shadow he was throwing on the dusty street. "I just wish you wasn't so damn *bright*, he said. "The old coal-oil lamps was plenty bright for me."

Slocum heard the hollow echo of boots on the sidewalk and turned to see a boy coming toward him with a wooden box in one hand and a pail in the other. Slocum doffed his hat and bowed elaborately. "Ah," he said. "the keeper of the merciless light."

The boy gave Slocum a wary look and pressed close to the store fronts as he passed by.

Slocum nodded. "I've been drinking," he murmured to himself. "I don't deny it. The honorable Judge Boyer says he's gonna cut loose an' have a good time."

The boy was climbing a ladder attached to the wooden pole supporting Slocum's street lamp. He climbed the seventy-five feet in less than a minute, inspected the carbons, and turned a knob that pulled them apart. In an instant the street below was almost as dark as Slocum's mood.

"Good time?" he said to himself. "Who the hell am I kidding?"

Slocum tried to see what the boy was doing on the ladder. Probably he was using a pair of pliers to pull out one or both of the hot carbon rods, which would have burned to a short length, and replacing them with new rods from the box. Slocum heard the clink of the old ones being tossed into the pail. A moment later the boy moved the two fresh carbons together so they touched. There was a crack and a fizzle when he eased them apart, just far enough to produce a new arc. It was even more brilliant than before. Slocum found himself in the center of a pool of light, casting a harsh and sinister-looking shadow on the sidewalk. The sight of it seemed to clear his head.

"I guess you're pretty far gone," he said to the shadow. "You didn't always talk to street lights, you know. Especially not when there was something constructive you could be doing."

Slocum was squinting against the glare of the light. Now his expression turned quizzical as he realized just how far gone he truly was. The day had been rough on him, of course. Shooting Will Church and seeing Susan Bently's reaction had dazed him. He remembered being questioned by the police chief, but only vaguely, as if it were an old dream. It seemed there had been a lot of shouting and accusations, but no arrest. Just as vaguely he remembered heading for a saloon the minute Boyer retired for the night. He couldn't remember eating anything.

The young light attendant had reached the bottom of the ladder. He jumped down from the third rung in youthful impatience, rattling his bucket of carbon rods, and marched off down the street toward the next high lamp. Showing almost as much purpose, Slocum moved in the opposite direction. He was thinking that the future belonged to young boys like the one he'd just seen—and like Pio Jameson. He was also thinking Pio might need the kind of help Slocum had to offer, if he was going to have a future.

It was over a beer and a pile of roast beef heaped on a slab of bread that Slocum learned the location of the whorehouse called the Rialto.

The Rialto was on the lower side of Los Angeles, near the little street they were calling Nigger Alley, but it turned out to be one of the fanciest brothels Slocum had ever seen. A rich-looking red wallpaper covered almost every inch of wall and ceiling that didn't hold silvered mirrors with ornate gilt frames or bawdy paintings and sculptures. A well-tuned piano was being played in another room, and everywhere he looked Slocum saw truly beautiful girls flirting with customers and serving liquor from crystal decanters. A willowy blonde wearing a low-cut gown and very little beneath it moved toward Slocum with a saucy, inviting grin. Slocum felt as if he were gawking at the way her full breasts and hips moved beneath the gown. This girl was even prettier than Susan Bently, and looked as if she had a lot more experience—not to mention simple animal hunger.

Slocum smiled at the blonde and said, "I sure hope your name is Louise,"

"I'm afraid not, stranger. But you can call me anything you want to."

"I'm afraid I need the real thing," Slocum said regretfully. "You do have a girl here named Louise, don't you?"

The blonde nodded her head, studying Slocum a moment

before moving up close to him. He could smell her hair, and feel the tips of her breasts rubbing against his chest.

"What is it with Louise?" the girl said. "What could she have that I don't have?"

"Probably not a thing," Slocum sighed. "But you know how it goes. A friend tells me I have to give her a tumble, and he won't stop raving about her until I do." He shrugged helplessly. "What can I do?"

"You tell me."

The blonde shifted her weight and Slocum felt her body moving against his. He sighed again and said, "Unfortunately, I can't disappoint a friend. But I can come back."

"You can probably even come more than once," said the girl, raising an eyebrow. "Especially if I'm taking care of you."

Slocum laughed. "Now that's what I call a winning slogan. Not that a girl who looks like you needs one. What's your name?"

"Melissa," said the blonde. "*Next* time just ask for Melissa." She hooked an arm through Slocum's and said, "Come on, you can wait inside." She led him through an arched doorway and toward a couch, catching the eye of the piano player. "Point out Louise to this gentleman when she comes down," the girl told the piano player. She gave Slocum one more wistful look and one more smile. "Don't forget," she said.

"Melissa," said Slocum. "How *could* I forget?"

He watched the fine roll of her hips as she walked away, longing to run his hands over the length of her body and hoping Louise wouldn't be too big a disappointment. He shook his head as if to clear it and glanced at the piano player to see if he was watching the girl, too.

He wasn't. He was rolling a fat cigar from one corner of his mouth to the other and eyeing Slocum with a suspicious expression. "Is this what it really looks like?" he said. "You passed her up, a girl like that, for another girl you ain't even seen yet?"

Slocum shrugged. "Friend's recommendation," he explained, even though it was sounding more lame each time he said it. "The way you're talking, I must have made a serious mistake."

The piano player looked down at his fingers for a little flourish in the tune he was playing. It was a cheerful ditty, and it had nothing at all to do with the suspicion in his eyes when he looked at Slocum again.

"Not necessarily a mistake," he said. "You sure as hell won't be disappointed. But I like it better when I know why a man does something."

"I told you why."

"Yeah. A friend told you."

The piano player was being sarcastic, and Slocum didn't blame him for being curious. But it also seemed like more than curiosity. Slocum took a closer look at the musician, who was about his own age, and noticed what seemed to be a bitter twist to the corners of his mouth. It looked as if the years had taken their toll on his face. It was fleshy and creased with deep lines, and his eyes were a flinty, cold blue.

"Where are you from?" said the piano player.

"Well," said Slocum. "The last place I was, was Oregon. I found out that hauling logs wasn't any kind of work for me."

The piano player laughed. "You got that right, Mr . . ."

"Slocum."

There was a flicker in those cold blue eyes. Slocum didn't think the man would make much of a poker player. It would have been a safe bet that the name meant something to him.

"Well, Mr. Slocum," said the other man, "I'm glad you came to your senses and found your way to Los Angeles." The blue eyes got cunning. "But I still can't figure why a smart man like you would turn his back on Melissa. You're buying a pig in a poke."

Slocum shrugged and changed the subject. "When it comes to jobs," he said, "I'd say you've got it pretty good yourself. Do you get to do more than just look as they go by?"

"There's some advantages here," the man said. "Oh, yes,

there are advantages." He grinned, and suddenly he looked like the kind of man who'd enjoy hurting a woman. Perhaps he'd found the only place where he could get what he wanted. Slocum felt sorry for the girls of the Rialto.

The harsh grin remained fixed on the piano player's face while he concentrated on his playing. Slocum stared at the ludicrous, frozen expression, finding it hard to connect with the light-hearted waltz music that was flowing from the man's fingers. Suddenly the piano player looked up, over Slocum's shoulder, and said, "Someone to see you, Louise."

Slocum turned and almost let his jaw drop open when he saw the red-haired girl towering above him. She was nearly six feet tall, but she wasn't heavy. Nor was she skinny. She had the kind of perfect figure that Slocum had only rarely seen—and there was just that much more of everything because of her size. Slocum stood slowly, almost respectfully, and found the top curls of her bright red hair at eye level. He didn't think his story of the friend's recommendation sounded so lame any more.

Louise looked from the piano player back to Slocum. "You asked for me?" she said softly. "How come?"

Slocum opened his mouth but heard the piano player's voice say, "A recommendation, honey—"

"And now I can see why," marvelled Slocum.

"I wonder if it's anyone you know," said the piano player.

The girl tilted her head to one side and smiled at Slocum, letting her eyes drift down over his body. "Yeah," she said. "Tell me who I have to thank for sending you over."

Slocum froze for an instant, then recovered. "I don't know what name he might use here," he said with a wink. "Married, you know."

"But not you, I bet."

Slocum shook his head. "Not for a long time, now."

The girl hooked her arms through one of his, as Melissa had—and Slocum was startled to realize he *had* forgotten Melissa, at least for the moment. He also found himself wondering about the owner of the Rialto, and the talent he had shown in setting the place up. Whoever it was had a superb taste in women. He was also no ordinary businessman.

Slocum paid with Judge Boyer's gold and was led upstairs to a plush room with a large, soft bed covered with pink pillows and pink satin sheets. Louise had not been cheap, but when he looked at it another way the price was a bargain. He was about to screw one of the most beautiful women he'd ever seen, and maybe—with any luck at all—trace down the rumor that was apparently destroying the Church and Jameson Bank.

Slocum was excitedly pulling off his pants when the name of the bank came to his mind. It brought to mind the image of Will Church's body lying on the boardwalk. Suddenly Slocum sat on the edge of the bed, his erection fading into nothing.

After a moment the redhead came around and sat beside him. She took one of his hands in both of hers, and when she asked what had happened, she seemed genuinely concerned.

Slocum looked down at himself and chuckled. "Don't take it personally," he said. "I was just thinking about something."

"It must have been pretty bad," said the girl. "What can I do?"

Slocum liked her concern. He liked the firm warm grasp of her hands around his, and the feel of her body beside him. "I think you're already doing it, Louise."

"Good," she whispered.

But the picture of Will Church was still there. Slocum brooded over it, and wondered why. He'd killed so many men in his life, but never anyone he'd liked so instinctively, or anyone as important as Will Church. Slocum had shot down one of the oldest and most respected figures in Los Angeles society. Perhaps worse, he had done it in the service of a man he disliked even more intensely than he'd liked Will Church. And Susan Bently had practically seen him do it.

Louise was beginning to stroke Slocum's thigh. She let her hand get tantalizingly closer all the time, and finally brought it home. But Slocum stayed mostly limp, even in her hand, as if something cut him off from feeling what the girl was doing. He looked sideways at her naked body, at the huge breasts hanging proudly between her arms, and still he felt almost nothing. Nothing more than a vague stirring.

Slocum met the girl's eyes and shrugged helplessly.

"You must have some pretty bad thoughts," she said with a sympathetic smile. As Slocum watched, the sympathy seemed to turn inward, to turn into sadness. "Isn't it terrible what your mind can do to you sometimes?"

"You, too?" said Slocum.

"Sure," the girl said gamely. "Look at the business I'm in."

Slocum nodded, and started thinking about the girl. He forgot about himself. Louise seemed to sense the change. She gave Slocum a promising smile and slipped off the edge of the bed to kneel before him, between his knees, leaning forward to cover his cock with her mouth. Slocum shivered in surprise and pleasure and immediately he began to swell inside her. She had to back off, Slocum's throbbing shaft sliding back out between her lips. It looked a little like some kind of private magic act, but Slocum didn't concentrate long on what it looked like. He only felt the wonderful pressure when she sucked, and the delicate bite of her teeth, and the feel of her lips sliding slowly up and down. Her tongue was busy, and so were both of her hands at the base of his erection. Now the girl was moaning softly as her head moved up and down. Slocum shivered again, fighting the new sensation that was like a fuse burning toward powder. How do you slow its rate? How do you keep the flame from reaching the powder without putting it out?

Slocum gave up trying. He wrapped his fingers in the mass of red curls before him and abandoned any control. In an instant he was bucking up and down and exploding in her mouth, which stayed with him to take everything he had to offer. She was moaning even louder as she swallowed and licked and swallowed some more. When he began to shrink again her lips moved closer and closer to the base of his cock, finally just holding it there lovingly. Slocum stroked the girl's soft red hair and let his hands slide down to caress her shoulders and arms. She squirmed beneath his touch like a contented cat hungry for affection.

"Now you've got me worried," Slocum said when he'd caught his breath.

Louise gently released Slocum from her mouth and looked up, frowning.

"You may have spoiled me for anyone else," Slocum continued. "It may be all downhill from here."

The girl grinned and began fondling him again. "I guess you'll just have to keep coming back," she said, and took a little nip at what she held in her hands. "Would that be so tough?"

"No," Slocum admitted. "You just may be seeing me again."

"It looks like the thought is already doing something for you."

Slocum had already felt the throbbing of blood rushing back to his groin, intensified now as Louise coaxed him with fingers and lips.

"I'm glad you've made another appearance," the girl said to Slocum's cock. "This one will be for me." She stood and before Slocum fully understood what was happening she had climbed onto his lap, spreading her legs straight and wide behind him on the bed. She was hanging onto his neck with one hand and with the other she was guiding his erection. She shifted her thighs a couple of times and suddenly Slocum felt himself deep inside her, hot and wet. He grasped her hips and helped her move while he thrust himself up and back, staring at the wonderful breasts that bobbed invitingly in front of his face, nearly filling his vision. He began kissing them, taking the nipples in his mouth and gently pulling at them. The girl responded by arching her spine, throwing her head back to make wild little sounds while Slocum moved faster beneath her.

"That's it," she suddenly gasped. "That's the rhythm. That's it! Oh yeah, that's *it!*" She was hugging Slocum's head with both arms in a ferocious grip. He felt as if he were smothering between her breasts, and loving every minute of it. He was moving faster and faster to meet the fury of her pumping thighs, her grip on his erection getting tighter and tighter. She hugged him harder, and Slocum enjoyed the squeeze of her breasts shifting against his cheeks. He clamped his fingers even harder on her sweat-dampened hips and their lust was almost a savage thing of violent thrusts and clenchings.

Slocum heard a cry, muffled slightly by the girl's breasts, and her fingernails dug into the flesh of his back as he felt her muscles convulsing all around him. Again he let himself go, surging into her at the instant that she stiffened and stopped breathing. They froze together for an instant, and then the room was filled with the sounds of two people fighting for air, gradually giving way to little sounds of satisfaction and contentment. They held each other for several minutes before the girl pulled away to look at Slocum, a liquid warmth in her eyes that gave Slocum a feeling like something was fluttering around in his gut.

"Lordy, mister," she said. "You sure got a way about you."

Slocum nodded his thanks and smiled. "I'd say that makes us even, Louise. I won't even mind paying for the extra time."

The girl rolled her eyes. "Are you kidding? I'd say that was *my* time we were on."

Slocum grinned. "Fair enough." He waited, expecting her to get up and get back to business. He was thinking about his own original business here, wondering how he would ask her about the Church and Jameson Bank rumors that four men said they'd heard from her. But Louise was lingering on his lap, her arms still around his neck, and there was a look of concern in her eyes.

"If you've got enough money to worry about," she said, "I hope it's in a safe place."

Slocum tried to hide his excitement with a breezy response. "Sure, it's in the bank. Until the next time I come to see you."

The girl flushed and looked down, her long delicate eyelashes brushing her cheeks. "That's not what I meant at all, John. I mean, *which* bank?"

"Well, at the moment it's in the Church and Jameson. But I've been out of town for a couple of weeks and now I'm hearing things that make me wonder."

"A good thing, too! Don't wait a day longer, John. Get down there first thing in the morning and get it back while you still can."

Slocum frowned. "But I wonder if it's really worth all the trouble," he said. "It's probably just a scare. These banks can take care of themselves."

"Most of the time, maybe. But not this bank."

Slocum gave Louise an intent look. "Are you saying something's really wrong with the bank?"

She nodded slowly. "I don't really understand it all, but it's something about the way the place is being run. I think there's going to be an audit, and when the results are known it'll mean the end of the Church and Jameson Bank. It might even mean some arrests."

"You're kidding!" Slocum said, genuinely surprised. "There's illegal things going on there?" Suddenly he frowned again, as if struck by a new thought. "Wait a minute," he said. "This sounds like something you're telling me from personal knowledge. How do you know all this?"

The girl blinked. "What do you mean?"

"I mean who told you this?"

She blinked again. "I don't know. It's just a rumor." Slocum held his eyes on hers until she looked away. "I just happen to know," she said.

"It'll be a lot easier to believe the rumor if I know the source, Louise. Who told you?"

"No one's ever asked me this before. I . . ." The girl looked around the room with an expression of confusion, then again looked at Slocum. "Just take my word for it, John. Please."

"I suppose it's better to play it safe," he said with a sigh. "But I'd feel better if I knew who told you all this. It almost sounds as if it was an officer of the bank, or at least someone who works there."

Louise looked even more confused. "It's just a rumor I heard somewhere," she said weakly.

"Now *that* I don't believe," Slocum said. "I guess it also bothers me that I think you're lying to me."

The girl looked troubled and dropped her eyes, running the fingers of one hand through the hair on Slocum's chest and watching the patterns she traced. "You're right," she said suddenly, as if hitting on a new idea. "It's a little more than just a rumor I heard. But you have to understand. It wouldn't be right to tell you how I know. It would be like breaking a confidence."

Slocum felt defeated. If he continued his pose as just another worried customer of the bank, he couldn't imagine any plausible way to pry out the girl's source. It even occurred to him that she *was* the source, knowingly or unknowingly spreading the rumor at the urging or on the order of Marcus Boyer or one of his agents. But, again, he felt he'd gone as far as he could go in the role he was playing. He had gone far enough, at least, to satisfy his hunch that the trail of rumors he was following would lead, ultimately, to Marcus Boyer—if Slocum really felt like pushing the matter. But he had never known what he would do with the information he was looking for, anyway. He figured he might as well let the whole thing go.

"Well," he said, easing Louise off his lap and onto her feet, "I think I'll play it safe and get there first thing in the morning. Thank you for the information."

Louise was looking worried, and he realized he'd sounded distant and formal. He smiled and winked at her. "I guess this time I got the tip instead of you," he said.

The girl laughed and seemed to relax. "We can try it the other way next time around," she said.

"Sure," said Slocum. "Next time."

She led him downstairs and gave his arm a squeeze as she said goodbye. Slocum smiled at her, and stopped smiling when he glanced over her shoulder and saw the piano player watching them closely. The short black cigar was still clenched between his teeth and there was the same cold look in his bright blue eyes. Slocum walked away from the Rialto with the piano player's expression in his memory and a queasy feeling in his gut.

Slocum remained uneasy as he walked through the dark city streets toward the Hotel Nadeau, and the feeling stayed with him as the elevator cranked its way slowly to the fourth floor. He waited near the cage after the elevator had returned to the lobby, but no one else came behind him and no one used the stairway at the other end of the hall. After a few minutes Slocum shrugged and ambled toward his room. The piano player's apparent recognition of John Slocum's name had spooked him, but when he passed the judge's suite he heard no sound coming from the room. Nor was there any light visible under the door. Still, Slocum was careful about entering his locked room. He slipped in quickly to flatten himself against the wall in the darkness, trying to sense any alien presence before he turned up the gaslight.

With the light turned up, Slocum glanced around his elegant, spacious room and shook his head, grinning. "I guess this ain't the old Wild West any more," he said aloud. "This here's the fine city of Los Angeles and I ain't got a thing to worry about, do I?"

The room seemed very quiet when Slocum finished talking to himself. He frowned at the dark window by his bed.

"Do I?" he repeated.

10

Slocum was never sure just what he was dreaming when the piano player entered his room. It might have been a bad dream, or perhaps it was only colored by the living nightmare it turned into.

Whatever the dream, it was invaded by the quietest of snicking sounds that almost didn't register. It was several seconds before some part of Slocum's mind recognized them as a key turning in the lock of his door, and several seconds more before he realized that he had lost some crucial time. A wild surge of fear coursed through his blood and his eyes popped open just in time to see a shadow gliding through the room. He caught the trace of a sour smell, like the odor of a stale cigar, but there was no time to think. The shadow came directly to his bed and raised its arm without any hesitation. There was the dull glow of steel above Slocum's belly and suddenly it was plunging toward him, again with a swiftness that caught Slocum by surprise. He was only just beginning to roll away from the thrust of the knife. He pushed so hard that he rolled off the bed, landing on the wooden floor with a loud thump.

Slocum tried to get up but he found that in rolling off the bed he'd wrapped the sheets around him. Now his arms were pinned at his side, useless, and the burly, dark form of the piano player was scrambling around the end of the bed with terrifying agility. Slocum pivoted on his back and kicked out at the man, but he was clumsy inside the sheets and couldn't connect. The piano player nimbly stepped out of his way, looking for an opening.

Slocum struggled to free his arms, and that gave the

piano player the chance he was waiting for. He lunged while Slocum was concentrating on his arms, and missed by little more than a foot when Slocum managed to roll away at the last instant. Again Slocum tried to kick, but he was wild with panic and his feet never touched the man.

The piano player didn't back off. Instead he circled away from Slocum's feet and toward his head for a better angle. Slocum knew he'd be done for if the man were successful. He'd never felt so helpless in his life. He rolled away again, but the sheets stayed wrapped around his body and the piano player simply shuffled after him. Slocum was sweating like a pig and it felt as if his straining heart would pound its way through his chest.

But the piano player was scared, too, now. He seemed desperate to get the job done and be gone and he didn't want to take any chances on leaving Slocum alive to get revenge. His pursuit was getting frantic, and Slocum's unpredictability was obviously making him nervous.

The hint of an idea came to Slocum and in the same instant he stopped rolling, partly on his side, apparently giving in to his helplessness. But as the piano player closed in Slocum jackknifed his legs up toward his chest in a great convulsion, sweeping the piano player's legs out from under him. The big man fell back with a loud noise and almost as he was going down, Slocum was struggling out of the tangled bedsheets and scuttling to his feet. He was as naked as the day he was born.

The piano player was up in the same moment, the knife still in his hand. The two men faced each other in the darkness and the only sound was their rough, jagged breathing. Neither of them said a word. The piano player tested Slocum with a few thrusts, but Slocum's reflexes were still sharp. He parried the thrusts and sidled away, trying to calm himself after the terror of helplessness. Except that now a black rage was building against the man who'd caused it. A moment before Slocum had wanted only survival. Now he wanted to kill the piano player. It was a savage, lustful feeling, and the piano player must have sensed it. Slocum saw him begin to falter, looking uncertainly toward the closed door and then trying to see the bureau and table and other furnishings in the room.

"That's right," said Slocum. "I've got a gun here somewhere."

The piano player jerked his head around, surprised to have his thoughts read so clearly.

"You won't find it," Slocum added. "But I will."

The frightened piano player lunged wildly and threw himself off balance. Slocum stepped in and smashed his jaw, but the man staggered back again out of reach, buying a little more time. Slocum tried to circle toward the bed and his gun under the pillow, but the piano player understood and cut him off.

Slocum figured it was just a matter of time before the piano player would get himself set again. He thought of the washstand in the corner behind him, with the towels on a hook above it. He backed up. The piano player followed. Slocum spun and grabbed for one of the towels, continuing the spin through a complete turn. The towel was only a vague shape in the darkness, but it felt solid in his hand. The piano player was already shuffling backward, but he wasn't fast enough. Slocum finished his spin with a snap of his wrist that slashed the end of the towel across the man's eyes.

The piano player grunted, both arms partially raised to try to ward off the blow. He was still backing up. Slocum had already grasped the other end of the towel with his left hand and now he stepped forward, bringing both ends of the towel down around the piano player's wrist. Each of Slocum's hands described a loop around the wrist, and in an instant the man's knife hand was trapped.

Slocum yanked the towel down, throwing the piano player off balance, and brought his elbow up for a smashing blow to the head as the other man fell forward. The piano player fell to his knees, but now it was his turn to panic. He used the momentum to tackle Slocum's legs with his shoulder, and Slocum wasn't balanced well enough to step out of the way. He stumbled backward, feeling the ends of the towel pulled from his grasp.

Slocum somersaulted backward and rolled to his knees, but the piano player had had enough. He was racing for the door. Slocum sprang up to catch him. The piano player already had the door open. He slammed it behind him and Slocum heard his running steps retreat down the hall toward the stairwell. Slocum had the door open only a few seconds later, ready to give chase, but a movement caught his eye in the other direction. He turned and was just in time to see Marcus Boyer's head disappearing back into his room. The door closed softly, followed by the loud click of a bolt being thrown into place.

Slocum froze for a second, considering the meaning of everything that had happened, and made a quick decision to retreat into his own room. He figured he had no way of knowing who else was in the judge's suite, or how many other murderers might be waiting to back up the fleeing piano player. It would be foolish to run out into the streets in nothing but his birthday suit, with no revolver or weapon of any kind. Slocum's burning desire to kill the piano player gave way to the dictates of common sense. It didn't occur to him as he dressed—his mind was too busy mapping the steps of the next few hours—but his ability to think clearly and make rational decisions, no matter what his state of mind, had been largely responsible for keeping him alive ever since he left Slocum's Stand to fight the Yankees.

Slocum had retrieved his Colt from beneath the pillow and kept it close by as he dressed. Now he carried it with him as he gathered up his few belongings around the room. He stuffed them in his old bag, so battered and stained by more than twenty years of hard travel, not to mention more than one of these hasty retreats. It seemed as if all the others came back to him now as he packed, listening every few seconds for the sounds of approaching danger, and a peculiar emotion stirred in his breast. It was a kind of emptiness. He tried to ignore it as he dumped half a box of shells into his jacket pocket. The box itself went on top of everything else in the bag. He closed it up and hefted it to his left shoulder.

There were still no sounds in the hallway. Slocum suddenly realized that he was probably not threatened from the direction of Boyer's suite, since the judge would not want to appear involved in the attempted murder—at least, not in any way that could be pinned down by the law.

Slocum slipped his Winchester out from behind the headboard of his bed and worked the action four or five times, ejecting the live rounds onto the crumpled sheets. When he satisfied himself that the carbine was working smoothly he reloaded the tube and made sure just once more that there was a round in the chamber. Then he made a final tour of the room, his Winchester in his left hand and the cocked Peacemaker in his right—both guns chambered for the .44-40's in his pocket—and eased himself into the hallway. Slocum's watch told him it was a little after two in the morning, which meant he'd been sleeping only an hour or so when the piano player tried to kill him.

I'm getting too old for these long nights, Slocum thought.

The hallway was apparently empty. It felt empty. Slocum sensed no movement or presence. But he kept the Winchester aimed down toward the elevator and the Colt up toward the stairwell as he sidled toward the judge's room with his back against the wall.

He stopped just to one side of Boyer's door, listening, but there was no sound behind it. He imagined the judge listening, too, perhaps just behind the door, only a foot or two away.

"I assume this means I'm fired," Slocum said loudly. He tried to imagine the judge's frustration and anger over the attempted assassination, and now his embarrassment. The thought made Slocum feel slightly better.

"Just remember money can't buy everything!" Slocum

yelled. "Sometimes it can't even buy a good murderer."

Slocum looked at the door and considered kicking it down. He wanted to smash it in and confront the sickly little man. But he had no idea what he would do then, and if he killed the judge he might well be charged with murder. He'd simply be repeating twenty-year-old history, exactly what he wanted young Pio Jameson to avoid. There was, too, the possibility that Boyer would already have another bodyguard inside. More than anything, however, Slocum wanted the judge to worry about what he might do. If Slocum had any luck at all, he would destroy the man slowly, with the chance to watch him suffer.

"This really isn't goodbye," Slocum finally said, in a cold, menacing tone. "I'll be seeing you again, *Your Honor*."

Slocum moved quickly back toward the stairwell and went down one flight at a time, listening intently on each landing and then racing down as fast as he could, but no one was waiting for him there. The lobby was empty except for the desk clerk, who dozed in a chair in the corner. He was a heavy old man with white hair, and he didn't seem even a little surprised when he woke up to find Slocum in front of him with a weapon in each hand.

"Something I can do for you?" he said mildly.

Slocum studied the man a moment. "You're not afraid of me, are you?"

"Me?" said the man, genuinely surprised. "Is there a reason I should be?"

"I don't know. Did you give anyone a key to my room tonight? That would be number—"

"Forty-seven. I know. But I didn't."

"Not even to my employer, the judge?"

"No, sir," said the clerk. "I been asleep right here. I didn't give him any keys tonight."

Slocum thanked the man and was turning away when he had second thoughts about his remarks.

"What do you mean, you didn't give him any keys tonight?" he said. "Did you give him a key some other time?"

"Well, sure," said the clerk. "He told me you agreed to it."

"When was this?"

"Last week, the night after you moved in. He said it was a safety precaution." Slocum scowled and the clerk looked concerned. "He told me it was okay with you, Mr. Slocum. He really did."

"I'm sure," Slocum said bitterly. "Don't worry. I realize you wouldn't have any reason to doubt the judge."

"Not up till now," the clerk said thoughtfully. "What happened up there, anyway?"

"Nothing that'll ever be made public. Nothing to worry about."

"A good desk clerk always worries," said the old man. He glanced at the bag slung over Slocum's shoulder. "I take it you're checking out?"

Slocum nodded. "You can still bill the judge. He'll be good for it."

The clerk studied Slocum with eyes that might have seen a lot of history in the West. He nodded after a moment, apparently reaching a conclusion. "I think I'll ask for some payment on account, just the same. In case something happens to the judge in the meantime."

Slocum let the hint of a smile appear on his face. "Not a bad idea," he said quietly.

"Just the voice of experience, young fella."

11

The gaslights were still burning behind their red-tinted windows at the Rialto whorehouse when Slocum arrived about two-thirty, straight from the Hotel Nadeau. He'd kept to the shadows like some of the other figures slipping furtively through the dark streets, staying alert but expecting no immediate trouble from Marcus Boyer. Slocum hoped he'd embarrassed the judge enough to keep him in his room for the time being.

But Slocum also had to face the fact that the judge wasn't easy to embarrass. He hesitated on the boardwalk across the street from the Rialto to think about it. If Boyer had guessed Slocum's next move, he might already be taking steps to head him off. Slocum stared at the whorehouse door for half a minute, chewing the inside of his lip, but he had no choice. He figured he was still better off acting as quickly as he could.

Slocum walked through the door of the brothel with the Winchester in his right hand and the Colt loose in its holster. No one met him in the parlor, but he heard the murmur of relaxed conversation in the next room. It seemed a good sign. When he passed through the arch he saw two girls curled up in overstuffed chairs and a third sitting at the piano. He didn't recognize any of them. They were watching him expectantly, with a bit of curiosity. The brown-haired girl at the piano said hello to Slocum and began picking out a tune with one finger.

"Sorry," he said shortly. "Looking for someone."

Slocum headed up the stairs he'd climbed with Louise

just a couple of hours before. One of the girls in the room behind him yelled "Hey!" Slocum ignored her. He heard all three of them on the stairs by the time he'd reached Louise's door. He tried the knob and threw the door open wide when he found it unlocked.

There was a lot of sudden motion on the big bed. A short and very fat man scrambled off the girl and crouched on the floor on the other side, trying to hide himself behind the mattress. "I didn't mean anything," he whined. "What do you want?"

"I sure as hell don't want you," said Slocum. He picked up a pile of the man's clothes that lay almost at his feet and tossed them over the bed. The three girls from downstairs crowded into the doorway behind him. "The party's cancelled," Slocum told the fat man, and jerked a thumb over his shoulder. "You can pick one of these three or get a refund. I don't care which."

Louise had backed herself against the headboard, a sheet pulled up to her chin. She was staring at Slocum, her big eyes filled with fear.

Slocum gave her a weak smile. "Whatever you think you know," he said, "you're wrong." He met her eyes and tilted his head to indicate the fat man, who was now rolling around on the floor beyond the bed, trying to slip into the clothes Slocum had tossed to him without exposing himself to the audience.

Louise grinned, then looked uncertainly at Slocum. "What *do* you want?" she said.

"To keep you alive, which may be a problem if my guesses are right."

"What are you talking about?"

Slocum tilted his head again, this time toward the three prostitutes looking on from the doorway. "Not in front of them."

The girl hesitated a moment, studying Slocum's face, then nodded at the other three. "He's all right," she told them. "I'll take my chances."

They didn't move.

"Really," said Louise.

The brown-haired girl who'd been sitting at the piano looked from Louise to Slocum. "If you say so," she said slowly. "But we won't be far away, honey." She turned her attention to the fat man, who was standing now and adjusting the clothes he'd put on while lying down. "Come on, Ernie," said the brown-haired girl. "We'll give you a good time."

The man named Ernie had regained a little composure along with his clothes. "It isn't fair," he complained. "I shouldn't have to pay anything after being interrupted like that."

"Don't worry," said the girl. "We'll make it up to you." There was a trace of resignation in her voice and Slocum wondered if they wouldn't resent him simply for the fact that now they had to take care of Ernie.

Louise, on the other hand, gave Slocum a dry smile when everyone else had gone. "Maybe I should thank you," she said. "He's one of the ones that give me the creeps."

"I'll bet," Slocum said. "What about Marcus Boyer?"

"Who?"

Slocum stared hard at the girl, but she didn't flinch. She only looked more perplexed. "You're telling me you don't know Judge Marcus Boyer?" Slocum challenged.

"A judge?" Louise said with a scowl. "Damn it, I thought I knew them all."

"Okay, I believe you."

"How wonderful!" the girl said sarcastically. "You break into my room when I'm doing business, and probably lose me a customer, just to say you believe me. You've really made my day, mister."

Slocum paced across to the bed and sat on its edge, not far from where he'd been the first time. But now there was a grim look on his face, and Louise was shrinking away from him again.

"Listen to me," he said, "your piano player tried to kill me tonight."

The girl covered her mouth with her hand. "That can't be," she said.

"You don't see him downstairs, do you? Let me tell you why. Less than half an hour ago he got into my room and came this far from sticking a knife in my belly."

"Oh, God."

"Now I'm going to do some talking and you're going to tell me if I'm right, okay?"

The girl nodded.

"First, it was the piano player who told you to spread that rumor about the Church and Jameson Bank. Right?"

The girl nodded again. "He told me it was just a business thing," she said pleadingly. "He said it was just a way to help a fellow out of a jam. I thought I was helping someone."

"That may be true," said Slocum. "It doesn't matter. What matters is that after I left tonight, the piano player... What's his name?"

"Weber. Mark Weber."

"After I left tonight, Weber asked you about me, didn't he?"

Louise nodded.

"And you told him about the questions I was asking about the rumors, didn't you?" Slocum went on.

"I never realized—"

"It doesn't matter, Louise. You told him what I said, and then he decided he had to go out."

The girl nodded again. "More or less," she said softly.

"Now let me tell you the facts," Slocum said. "Or the facts as near as I can come so far. When this bank scare hit, a man named Marcus Boyer loaned the Church and Jameson Bank six hundred thousand dollars to help them—"

"Six hundred thousand!" Louise said in awe.

"That's right. And supposedly to protect himself he made the owners sign mortgages on all their land. It amounts to two large ranches and several blocks of prime lots here in town, and it's worth at least four times the six hundred thousand."

There was a flicker in the girl's eyes. "So that's it."

"I guess you already see where I'm going," Slocum said, letting his tone show that he was impressed. "If I've got it figured right, Boyer told the piano player to start a rumor through the Rialto. He picked you, probably because you have more customers than any other three of these girls." Louise smiled and lowered her eyes. "There's also the fact that you're likely to appeal to the people with a little extra money," Slocum continued, "the kind who'd have money in the bank and know other people in the same position. This is a perfect place to start a rumor, and no one could tie it in to the judge." Slocum gave her a moment to let it all sink in, then added, "Except you and Weber."

The girl's eyes went wide. "You mean—"

"With both of you around," said Slocum, "there's a direct line back to Marcus Boyer. Just two links in the chain. The chain is broken if *either* of you gets taken out of the picture."

The girl's eyebrows furrowed heavily as she stared at the floor. She nodded her head. "I see it," she said slowly. "And I see that I'd be the first to go. I'm probably the expendable one." Suddenly her eyes focused on Slocum. "If you're telling me you'll help me get away," she said bluntly, "I'm asking you why."

Slocum had been ready to mention their session earlier in the evening, as if it was a sentimental gesture, but something in the girl's look made him want to tell the whole truth. He'd also decided she was too smart to be fooled for long. "It's a long story," he said finally. "But the thing of it is, I want to make sure the Jameson family doesn't lose their land."

"What could I do?"

"Testify, for one thing. No court would let Boyer exercise his mortgages if we could prove fraud."

"You're not serious! He'd want me dead even worse than he does now."

"It's a risk. You can go it alone, if you want."

"But it wouldn't do any good. I can't pin it on Boyer. I

never even heard his name before tonight," she protested.

"You could pin the tail on Weber, though, and he might be willing to talk about the judge just to save his own skin."

"I'd still be a sitting duck, damn it. I'd be a dead one."

"Not if I can help it. And don't forget the family I'm talking about. They have I don't know how many acres out there. I think they'd turn out to be pretty grateful."

"I don't know," said Louise. "Maybe."

Slocum held up his hand and they both heard the sound of excited voices coming from down below. A moment later they heard the urgent pounding of boots on the stairs. It sounded like at least two men, maybe three.

"Oh God," said the girl."Yes, John. *Yes!*"

Slocum laughed and said, "Quiet, Louise. Someone might think there was something going on in here." He leaped toward the door and threw the bolt home just before the approaching men halted on the other side. Someone tried the latch and then the piano player's voice said, "Are you all right, Louise?"

"Of course, Mark. What's wrong?"

She was out of bed, slipping into a pair of riding jeans. Her breasts bounced between her arms as she pulled the denims over her hips. Slocum had to force himself to keep his eyes on the door.

"You can't trust that man," the piano player was yelling. "Don't listen to a word he tells you."

The girl hesitated, then winked at Slocum. "How would you know he was telling me anything, Mark?"

"Let us in," said the piano player. "We'll take care of you." Someone tried the latch again, and someone else started pounding on the door. The girl was putting on an old grey shirt, stretching the fabric tight across her chest to fasten the buttons. She pulled open one of the drawers in her bureau, reaching inside with one hand and beneath it with the other. She came up with a taped envelope and a little pepperbox gun.

"This is how much I trust you," Louise whispered, with

a twinkle in her eye. "My savings are in the envelope, and the gun is . . . just in case."

Slocum brushed it aside. "Any other way out of the room?" he asked.

Louise shook her head.

"Damn!"

"Let us in!" the piano player yelled again. Slocum flexed his fingers around the butt of his Colt. He thumbed back the hammer on his Winchester. The pounding of fists gave way to the thud of a body slamming against the door. Slocum backed away a foot or two, intent on the opening.

"Don't try it!" Louise yelled suddenly. "Slocum has a gun on me!"

The pounding stopped and Slocum snapped his head around to look at the girl. She shrugged modestly, dipping her head in silent urging to carry through with the idea.

"You heard her," Slocum said. "Make a bad move and you lose your star attraction."

There was a whispered conversation on the other side of the door. Slocum smiled at Louise and snarled, "I'll kill her if I have to."

"No, no," said the piano player. "What do you want?"

"Safe passage."

"That's all?"

Slocum frowned in concentration. "You got a horse?" he asked.

"Does that mean you're getting out of town, Slocum?"

"The sooner the better."

"Just one horse? What about the girl?"

"I'll drop her as soon as I'm clear."

There was more whispering on the other side of the door. Louise flashed a worried look at Slocum, who shook his head. "Throw a few things in a bag," he said softly. "Just the bare essentials. Do it fast."

The girl nodded her understanding, but still looked worried.

"We'll get clear," Slocum murmured. "You're not the

only one with ideas, and I've been at this sort of thing for a long time."

"I suppose," she whispered, gathering clothes from her drawers. "But I thought you said they wanted to kill me anyway."

"Exactly," said Slocum. "That's why we—"

"All right," yelled the piano player. "Give us ten minutes. You'll find a little quarterhorse out front."

"No tricks?"

"You won't be bothered, Slocum. Not unless you try any funny stuff—or try coming back to Los Angeles."

"You got a bargain," said Slocum. "Now get the hell out of here."

He listened to the shuffle of their boots in the hallway and on the stairs. He heard a short conversation down below, then the sound of the front door being opened and closed. Slocum motioned Louise to duck behind the bed, silently easing back the bolt on the door. He whipped it open and stepped into the hall with his Colt in front of him. The hall was empty. He cocked his head, listening to the sounds in the rest of the building. Finally he nodded toward Louise and said, "Come on."

She stood and came toward him slowly, looking confused. "I thought they said ten minutes."

"That's why we're leaving now."

"But what about the horse?"

"They'll be watching it, of course, and they'll kill us both for stealing it. They might even call in a little law to make it look right. But while they're watching the horse, we'll be disappearing out the back door. You *do* have a back door, don't you?"

The girl's look of confusion had turned into a smile, and now she laughed outright. "Ladieeeees and gentlemen," she said, "keep your eyes on my right hand. It won't have a thing to do with what's about to happen."

Slocum smiled and raised one eyebrow. "Let's just hope they believe in magic," he said.

12

"I can see why the widow and her son want to keep this place," said Louise.

"It's not just the orange groves and the cattle," said Slocum. "They've also got their own water, in the arroyo up there above the house."

"Someone did a good job of laying it out. Counting the water rights, this place must be worth a fortune."

"Yeah, but how do they protect it from the likes of Marcus Boyer?"

The girl shook her head sadly and ran a hand through her hair. It felt tangled and gritty after the hours of hard riding from Los Angeles. Slocum had insisted on carefully selecting the horses they stole, looking for speed and durability even though there had been almost none to choose from on the city streets when they fled the Rialto. Slocum had sold his own mount in Portland before he boarded the train for Los Angeles, and he hadn't seen much point in buying another one since he'd arrived. Sometimes he remembered when a horse had been an absolute necessity to a man in the West, one of the needs that distinguished him. But the West was changing fast.

Slocum had also insisted on a punishing pace, so that by dawn they were settled in behind the crest of a low hill above Maria Jameson's garden, waiting for the Rancho Cabrillo to come to life.

"I'm glad we made it," Slocum said. "Even if we won't be walking quite the same for a while."

"If ever," Louise groaned. She stretched her legs and

massaged the muscles in her thighs. "Will the overseer really get out of the house?"

"I hope so," Slocum said grimly. "That's his job, anyway—to keep an eye on what goes on around here—and he seemed like the kind of man who would do his job. So when he goes out, we go in to talk to the Jamesons about rumors."

"You think the overseer would make trouble for us?"

"When he found out what was going on he would. But I don't even want the judge to know we're out here."

"I'll go along with that."

They waited a while in the silence of the desert, the red sun drifting up over the rim of the mountain wall behind them. There was the fresh smell of sage in the air, and the bite of lingering dust. The sound of their own breathing seemed loud in the stillness.

They had waited nearly an hour when they noticed movement and saw a tall, lean figure slip from the ranch house toward a corral attached to the back. A moment later the figure rode out on a handsome grulla, and Slocum recognized it as the horse Pio Jameson had been riding on the first day he'd seen him. Slocum also recognized the fine horsemanship. "That's the boy," he told Louise. "It has to be Pio. There aren't many men who can ride the way he does."

"What do you think he's doing?"

"I was hoping you wouldn't ask," Slocum said with a frown. "I don't have any ideas on that score."

"He keeps looking over his shoulder, doesn't he?"

"So it appears. I wonder if he's trying to give Pierce the slip."

"The judge's overseer? Why would he do that?"

"Another good question. I'm thinking we should find out."

They mounted their horses and paralleled Pio Jameson's trail, using the cover of ridges and small washes that crisscrossed the land. They travelled slowly to keep the dust down. But the boy was looking for pursuit from the ranch headquarters, and he didn't pay much attention to anything else. Louise and Slocum were able to follow him from a distance, up into the foothills of the towering San Gabriels. They had gone about four miles in a little less than an hour when the rider angled toward a grove of oak trees that filled a cleft in the mountain. The dusty green of the oaks still looked very bright against the pale brush and sand around it. Slocum guessed there was a spring there. He pulled up to study the grove and heard shots coming from down below.

"Oh, shit," he said. He kicked his horse into a run down the slope, Louise right behind him, but after a few seconds he skidded to a stop again and held up his hand. "That sounds like it's all coming from the same gun," he told the girl. "And listen to the way it's spaced. I think our boy is practicing."

Pio Jameson had ridden into a small clearing in the grove and immediately drawn his gun, a four-inch Smith and Wesson revolver, choosing his target as he drew. It was a small tin can, one of many on the ground left behind from previous sessions like this. The boy's slug exploded the gravel about two inches to the left of the can.

"God damn it," he said.

Pio Jameson swung a leg over his pony's neck and slid off the saddle, firing again as he hit the ground. He was still an inch to the left. Pio emptied his revolver in frustration, hitting the can once. There was a brooding look on his face as he dug into his saddlebag for a handful of shells to reload his gun. He put it back in the holster and took a deep breath, then another. Almost without planning to, he let his hand sweep up in a fast draw. The gun came clear. He fired. The can danced away. Pio smiled a moment, then frowned. He knew the draw had been slow, and he had felt it to be awkward. He tried again, slowing it down even further to think about each movement, then slowly speeded up the movements as he felt the smoothness returning. He reloaded a second time, flexed his fingers, and continued with his practice. He aimed for different cans, at different distances and heights in front of him. His accuracy slowly improved.

Pio Jameson reloaded a third time, then a fourth. The fifth time around, he had just ejected the spent shells from the cylinder when he heard Slocum's voice behind him. "You're not moving your hip, Pio," Slocum said.

The boy spun around, instinctively raising the gun as if it could fire with its cylinder swung open. His eyes showed fear and panic, even though Slocum was alone and standing there with his thumbs hooked over his belt. He had left Louise farther back in the trees, waiting for a signal. Slocum had figured she would be nothing more than a distraction while he was first trying to gain Pio Jameson's trust. The boy might worry about saving face before such a beautiful woman, and be reluctant to accept anything Slocum had to say about the judge's intentions for Rancho Cabrillo.

"That's another thing," Slocum said calmly. "If you're expecting any kind of trouble, never let yourself get caught with an empty gun."

Pio Jameson suddenly came to life, shoving cartridges into the cylinder.

"Now, don't do anything stupid, either," Slocum warned. "I'm not working for the judge any more."

The boy glanced suspiciously at Slocum and kept loading, but there was a little less urgency about his actions.

"I could have killed you a hundred times over," Slocum said impatiently. "That's not why I'm here." He decided to bluff it through, pacing toward the boy and talking as though everything was settled. "Here, let me show you what I mean," he said, stopping just in front of Pio. "One of the things that's slowing you down is getting the barrel clear of your holster. You have to lift the gun too high, and that's costing you valuable time."

Pio Jameson's distrust was mixed with confusion now. He was listening to Slocum and watching his demonstration, but he wasn't sure what to make of it.

"Now watch me," Slocum was saying. "I'll do it slowly at first. See the way my hip is kind of dipping down, going the opposite direction of my hand? It's all happening at the same time. By doing both things at once, I'm getting the gun clear almost twice as fast. You can't afford any wasted effort. Now you try it."

Pio Jameson looked hard at Slocum, still perplexed. But Slocum's gun was safely back in its holster, and his thumbs were back in his belt. Slowly the boy turned away, his hips twitching from side to side as he familiarized himself with the muscles he would be using. At first he simply moved them in unison with the motion of his hand, practicing the coordination. It didn't come easily.

"Try bending your legs more at the knees," Slocum suggested. "Give yourself more room to move."

Again there was that perplexed look, Pio Jameson wondering why his former enemy should want to offer this advice. But the words made sense, so he tried again. He began to draw without firing, doing it over and over until it felt more natural. Finally he set himself in the familiar gunfighter's stance, staring fixedly at one of the tin cans before him. He drew and fired. Slocum didn't see any cans get hit, but a wide grin appeared on Pio's face just the same.

"Yes!" he said happily. "It feels much better. Much faster. I didn't hit the can, but if I work on my speed, the accuracy will take care of itself."

"No," said Slocum. "Work on them together. Speed is good, but not if you miss the first time. Sometimes you don't get another chance. The important thing is to make sure the first bullet counts."

Pio Jameson's grin disappeared as quickly as it came, replaced again by dark suspicion. "Why do you tell me this?" he said. "How did you find me?"

"I followed you from the ranch, Pio, and I'm here because I don't want to see you lose it."

"Why is that your concern?"

"Because I'm making it my concern."

"But why? Is it revenge, perhaps? Has the judge fired you?"

"You might say that," Slocum said with a grin. "He tried to have me killed last night."

"Why?" Pio said again.

"Because I found out that he's behind the rumors that are causing so much trouble for the bank. Some of them, at least."

"I thought as much," Pio said fiercely. "That's why I will kill him."

"Killing him isn't the answer," said Slocum.

"I cannot allow him to steal my mother's land."

"I understand that, Pio. But killing Marcus Boyer will only bring you more trouble than you already have. Believe me."

"You talk like an old man," the boy said scornfully.

Slocum's face hardened for a moment, then softened into a wry smile. "I guess I do. It's true I've lived many more years than you. But in all those years I've *learned* a few things, Pio. It's a question of experience, and I've had a hell of a lot more of that than you have."

The boy blinked a couple of times, apparently thinking about what he'd heard, and Slocum was surprised despite himself. He wasn't so sure that he would have listened to anyone at that age. Maybe the kid was smarter than he had been. At least he seemed smart enough to listen.

"I suppose you have a better idea?" Pio challenged.

"That's right," Slocum said calmly. "Are you willing to listen?"

The boy hesitated, then spoke stiffly. "My mind is open."

"Very good," said Slocum, and he felt a warm glow of pleasure that was something like pride. He could not have wished more from his own son if he'd had one. As it was, there was no one to benefit from his years of hard living. Sometimes, when he let himself think about it, Slocum was saddened by the fact that all his knowledge of weapons and trails and weather and horses would disappear when he died. It didn't seem right. He felt as if the things he knew should be passed on to someone else. Slocum's life would have a little more meaning if, because of it, someone else avoided his painful mistakes and learned things he himself had learned the hard way.

"Very good," Slocum said again, and whistled a shrill note. "I have someone I want you to meet," he said. "A prostitute from Los Angeles. She is the one who kept the rumors going, telling her customers that the Church and Jameson Bank was badly managed."

Louise came through the trees, leading their stolen horses, and Pio kept looking back and forth from her to Slocum. His expression was one of bafflement, but his widened eyes also showed the effect her size and beauty had on him. "Why would she do that?" he demanded.

"You told him?" Louise asked Slocum, and when he nodded she explained her instructions from Mark Weber, the piano player. "I thought maybe it was true," she finished. "I guess I wanted to think I was helping people. And it never . . . I never let it occur to me that I might be hurting someone."

Pio Jameson gave her a dark, hooded look and turned to Slocum. "How did you find out?" he asked. "An accident?"

"Not at all." Slocum began telling Pio about his trip to the bank and his efforts to trace the damaging rumors back to their source. He described his visit to the Rialto, and the attempt on his life, although he didn't go into much detail about being tangled up in his bedsheet. "The fact that Boyer tried to have me killed must have meant I was close to exposing him, Pio. When I realized that, I knew Louise had to be the one behind the rumors. I decided to get her out of the Rialto, in case the judge wanted to eliminate the connection. I also figured she might be able to help you out."

Pio was shaking his head. "You still haven't explained something, Mr. Slocum. You had no obligation toward us.

There is no bond of friendship. You could have simply disappeared last night. Why didn't you?"

Slocum sighed deeply and looked at Louise, who clearly wanted to hear the answer just as much as Pio did. "My family once owned some of the choicest land in Georgia," he said. "A long time ago. Then came the War between the States. My brother was killed in the fighting, and my parents died, too." Pio and Louise looked sympathetic. "The thing is, I still had the farm. We called it Slocum's Stand. It would have flourished under my brother's hand, but I figured I could do well enough. After the War all I wanted was to find a wife and make a home there. Then a man in the new government—he was a judge, too—he decided he was going to have the farm. He claimed we hadn't been paying taxes."

"Could he really get away with it?" Louise said.

"I thought he could," said Slocum, "just like Pio here thinks Boyer will get away with his mortgage scheme. I figured the damn carpetbaggers could do anything they wanted, and the only thing I could do to keep the judge from having my land was to kill him."

"Did you?" breathed Pio.

Slocum nodded sadly. "I shot him down, in a fair fight. And then I burned my place to the ground."

Louise gasped audibly, and Pio looked horrified. "Why?"

Slocum fixed the boy with a steady stare. "Do you really think they'll leave you alone here if you kill the judge, Pio? Do you really believe you'll be able to ride back here and continue running the ranch as if nothing had happened?"

"If it's a fair fight," Pio stammered. "If I make sure—"

"Damn it, the judge will make sure it's *never* a fair fight. Haven't you figured that out yet? He won't face you himself. He'll have men around who will do his fighting for him. Or they'll kill you in your sleep, the way he tried to do me. He won't stand there and wait for you to draw like something in a penny dreadful."

"I suppose not."

"Of course not. You'd have to shoot him down, and the law won't stand for that. You'd be on the run. Your whole life would be changed, not to mention what your mother's life would be like without you. You'd probably never see her again. Or the ranch."

Pio was staring off into the trees, but Slocum could see that even the thought of leaving the ranch behind was a kind of torture. Pio turned to Slocum and said, "What happened for you?"

"I ain't seen the home place in more than twenty years, Pio. I also haven't known a whole lot of peace in that time. Once you get on the wrong side of the law it's hard to get back. Sometimes I think . . . Well, if I'd done things different, maybe I could be there right now. Maybe I'd be wakin' up next to a wife, with a couple of sons already up and doing the chores, knowing the place would be theirs one day."

Slocum suddenly had to stop talking. He blinked his eyes against the moisture he felt there, and was embarrassed when Pio's gaze dropped to the ground. Louise moved closer and took his arm.

"Perhaps not," Pio said softly, still staring at the ground. "What if the judge had succeeded? Perhaps nothing would be different today. You can't know what would have happened the other way."

"But I didn't try," Slocum said. "I went off like some half-cocked fool and did the first thing that came to my mind. I didn't even *try!*"

"I understand," Pio said, nodding slowly. "But how can I fight Boyer?"

"The law, Pio. The courts."

The boy laughed bitterly. "The courts," he repeated. "Marcus Boyer bought the courts when he bought his title. It's hopeless."

"No, it's not."

Pio snorted.

"All right," Slocum sighed, "it might turn out to be a

dead end. But what do you lose by trying? You lose *everything* if you kill the judge."

Pio Jameson studied Slocum. "What do you propose?" he finally said.

"A deposition," Slocum said immediately. "That's why I brought the girl. I'm sure your family has a good lawyer. Get him to take a statement from Louise, and use it as he sees fit. He can probably get the mortgage set aside, or at least make it so your mother can pay off her share."

"What about Mr. Church?"

Slocum's face fell. "You haven't heard?"

"Heard what?"

Slocum took a deep breath. "He's dead, Pio. He made me kill him last night, after we got back from your ranch."

"*Made* you kill him.?"

"I tried everything. But he was aiming at the judge and his finger was closing on the trigger. I had no choice."

Pio's eyes were glittering. "You could have let him do it."

"I, too, am a man of honor. It was still my job to protect the judge."

Pio stared hard at Slocum for a minute, then slowly he nodded. "I can understand," he said softly. "And I can remember that you didn't kill me even when you had the chance, and the excuse."

"Then you'll try it my way?" said Slocum. "You'll give the law a chance to handle Marcus Boyer?"

"Yes," said Pio, almost fiercely. "We will try it your way—for now."

"I don't think so," said a voice behind them.

It was the man named Pierce. He was standing behind a tree at the edge of the clearing, his new Winchester trained in their direction. "I think the judge would rather see you first, boys. And from what I've been hearing, Slocum, he's going to be particularly happy to see you and the girl again."

13

"You're on the wrong side in this fight," said Slocum.

"You might be right," said Pierce. "But it's like you was telling the boy. I took the judge's money. So you take your turns dispensing with the hardware, nice and easy. You first, Slocum."

Slocum used his left hand to slide the Colt out of its holster and place it gently on the ground. He was straightening up when, from the corner of his eye, he saw Pio's boots shifting in the dust as the boy settled himself.

"No," Slocum said quietly. "Don't try it, Pio."

The man named Pierce glanced at Slocum and then took a closer look at Pio. "Get rid of that gunbelt," he said tensely.

Pio Jameson didn't move.

"Do it," said Slocum. "This isn't the time."

"There won't *be* a time if we don't have our weapons, Slocum," said the boy.

Pierce lifted the rifle to his shoulder and sighted down the barrel on Pio's chest. "Damn it, boy, drop that gun!"

Pio still didn't move. There was a dead stillness in the oak grove.

"He'll kill you," Slocum murmured. "The man knows what he's doing with that Winchester."

Pio's stare was glassy-eyed, as if he'd gone a little out of his head. "You tell me the girl's testimony is our last chance," he said to Slocum. "How can I let him take her to the judge?"

"It's a long way to Los Angeles, Pio. You gotta play the

odds." Slocum could see Pierce's chest rising and falling. The overseer was keying himself up to a fever pitch. He was blinking rapidly and sweat was forming on his forehead. Slocum watched the man's trigger finger and tried to keep his voice calm. "You're making it worse, Pio. He's gonna shoot now if one of the horses decides to take a shit. For Christ's sake, drop the gunbelt. *Think about your mother!*"

The glaze left Pio's eyes and he seemed to see Pierce for the first time. He nodded and let his hands drift away from his sides. "I'll do what you say," he told the gunman. Like Slocum, he kept his right hand away from his side and used his left to unbuckle the gunbelt. He let it fall to the ground. Slocum closed his eyes in relief, and he heard an audible sigh from Louise. Pierce wiped his forehead with a big hand.

"That was smart," Pierce said. "Stay that way and no one will get hurt."

"Until Marcus Boyer gets hold of us," Slocum snapped. "Then he'll kill the girl and me and ruin this boy's life."

"That ain't my affair, Slocum. My job is just to keep an eye on what happens around the ranch."

"The hell it ain't your affair. You're just as guilty as if you shoot us right here and now."

"Don't think I ain't thinkin' about it!" the man blustered, shifting his rifle uncomfortably. "You just keep your mouth shut and your hands where I can see 'em."

"Sure," said Slocum, "I'll keep my mouth shut. But you can't ignore the things your head is telling you."

Pierce jerked his rifle around in Slocum's direction and said, "God damn it, I told you to shut up."

"Sure, Pierce. What did you do, follow the boy's tracks out here?"

"Slocum . . ."

"Okay," said Slocum. "I can take a hint. It's just that I feel bad the girl trusted me enough to leave with me." Louise had been watching him with an expression that was getting more and more puzzled. "If she hadn't *trusted* me," Slocum said significantly, "she might not be in this fix."

"Don't worry about it," the girl comforted him, but there was the glimmer of an idea in her eyes. Slocum hoped she was thinking about the previous night when she had showed him the little pepperbox from her bureau drawer, the little four-barreled gun she said she'd keep with her "just in case."

Pierce was staring at Slocum and the girl in frustration. "Just get on your damn horses," he finally said, swinging the barrel of his rifle. "And no funny stuff. I can make this thing hit what it's aimed at up to a hundred yards. Sometimes more, when I get lucky."

The overseer was not just lucky, but smart and thorough. He carefully searched each saddle and anything he found on it, removing Slocum's Winchester as well as the little Remington derringer he found in Slocum's bag. Then he studied each of the men for telltale bulges, ordering them to lift their trouser legs so he could check for weapons that might be hidden in the tops of their boots. Pierce was eyeing Louise—and Slocum was getting nervous—when the girl smiled and started moving toward the overseer.

"I suppose you'll want me to take everything off," she taunted.

Pierce licked his lips.

"Otherwise you'll never know just what's under all these clothes."

"Well . . ."

Pio Jameson had a dark scowl on his face, showing his disgust for the whore, and Slocum remembered what it was like always to be jumping to conclusions. It was painful, usually, and sometimes embarrassing. Slocum was watching the girl and the overseer, ready to take advantage of whatever might happen.

"I have an even better idea," Louise purred when she was standing in front of Pierce. "Why don't we just kind of stroll off into the trees, where no one can watch."

Pierce snorted and said, "Who'd be left to watch? Your friends here would get clean away." He was trying to keep his rifle between himself and the girl, but it must have seemed impolite to point a gun at a girl who was talking to him like that. She put her left hand on the overseer's chest and started playing with his shirt buttons.

"Is that so terrible?" she said. "You don't really want to take them in anyway, do you?"

The rifle wavered a little, but Pierce said, "It's my job, ma'am."

Louise let her hand slide down the man's shirt front until her fingers slipped over and behind his belt buckle. Slocum repressed a smile, wondering if Pierce could feel the warmth of her hand through his shirt, just a few inches from his groin. Slocum didn't envy the overseer's position. Louise gave a little tug, as if using the belt to draw herself closer. The tips of her breasts grazed Pierce's chest.

"I've sure got a hankering," Louise said. "And you look like the man to take care of it."

She had gone too far. Slocum saw clarity return to Pierce's eyes. "Go try that line on the kid," he said harshly. "I've been around too long to be fooled by a bitch like you." He yanked her hand out of his pants and pushed it away violently.

The force of the shove made Louise spin around. She stumbled and fell, collapsing in the dirt in a pile of legs, arms, and clothes. Slocum leaped forward as if to help her, but Pierce swung the barrel of his rifle to cover Slocum. Louise immediately unscrambled herself. In one hand was her pepperbox.

"Don't move an inch, you bastard."

Her tone told all three men that she'd had trouble with their kind before. Pierce instinctively began to swing back, then froze. He and Slocum both noticed that the girl was trembling violently, a reaction to her fear. "I ain't movin' an inch," Pierce stammered. "You just be careful with your finger on the trigger."

Slocum relieved the overseer of his collection of weapons, most of which went in Slocum's bag or on his saddle.

He returned Pio's Smith and Wesson and then went to stand in front of the girl. She was still on the ground. Slocum held out a hand to help her up.

"You!" she said, pointing the gun vaguely in his direction. "If it hadn't been for you, I wouldn't be in this mess."

"You were already in it," Slocum said quietly. "If it weren't for me, you'd probably be dead already. Here, let me help you."

Louise yanked her arm away. Slocum shrugged. He understood the effects of fear. He wasn't angry, but he didn't know what else to say. Pio appeared beside him, looking gravely down at the girl.

"I have an apology," he said.

Louise looked at him, surprised. "You didn't do anything."

"For my thoughts," the boy said gravely. "I misjudged you badly just now, and I am very sorry." He reached for her arm with remarkable assurance, and the girl let herself be lifted to her feet. She was still trembling. Pio put his arms around her and squeezed tight. "You did a wonderful thing," he murmured. "You saved us."

The girl began crying, pouring tears onto Pio's chest. "I was so scared," she said.

"I know." Pio stroked her hair. "I know how it is to be scared."

Louise kept sobbing, her breath catching in her throat, and Pio soothed her as best he could. Slocum watched him, and thought he was doing *too* damn good. But then he knew that Pio was not truly a boy. He was probably only a year or two younger than Louise, and just as tall. Slocum grimaced. He had to admit they made a nice-looking couple. He was not the type to wish the life of a whore on anyone. It was just that you didn't meet many whores like Louise. It would be a real loss to Los Angeles and the profession.

Slocum sighed and began to get Pierce ready for traveling.

• • •

Maria Jameson was once again irrigating her garden when the little party rode up to the headquarters of the Rancho Cabrillo. She shaded her eyes with her hand and watched them approach, and there was a certain rigidness to her body that looked like fear. Slocum remembered that she knew nothing of his switch in allegiances. Pio was apparently just remembering the same thing.

"Everything is all right," he called out to her. "We have new friends, and this man is our prisoner."

Maria Jameson put down her shovel and came to hear the story Pio had heard only an hour earlier from Slocum and Louise. Slocum was afraid the proud ranch owner would scorn the prostitute, but he was wrong. Maria studied Louise for a moment, made some mysterious feminine judgement, and that was the end of it.

"We are grateful to you both," she said simply. "We will be deeply in your debt. Pio, show them where to wash and find fresh clothing. We will have a fine dinner, and then you can rest."

"Uh... there's one thing more," Slocum said. "We'll have to get these horses off your ranch. They aren't exactly ours."

There was a glint of amusement in Maria Jameson's eyes. "You will not worry about such small matters," she said. "One of our men will take them down and turn them loose in the arroyo. They will find their way home."

Slocum was glad to let the woman take care of things. He was feeling the effects of his drunken, almost sleepless night, and the lack of any food since the saloon sandwich of the night before. Maria Jameson began shouting orders in Spanish and tall, dark-skinned men appeared from the house as if by magic. Pierce was taken off to be locked in a room until it could be decided what to do with him. The two stolen horses were led away. Slocum's bag was taken to a guest room. And Pio himself went with Louise to show her where she would stay. Slocum remained with Maria, smiling inwardly. Pio hadn't been able to take his eyes off the girl since they'd left the oak grove. For her part, Louise seemed to enjoy Pio's talk and his laughter. They were of the same age, and the same flashing temperament. Pio's mother watched the two of them until they disappeared into the house. Then she turned back to Slocum and gave him a direct, knowing look.

"You have been with that woman?" she asked.

There were polite evasions on the tip of Slocum's tongue. He looked into Maria Jameson's dark clear eyes and said, "Yes. One time."

"Is she a good woman?"

Slocum glanced at the house, thinking of the girl's concern for him that didn't seem entirely motivated by financial reward. He also thought of the way she had gamely followed him through the long, hard night, making fun of her discomfort if she complained at all. Slocum smiled and said, "I am only a man, but I would say she could make your son very happy."

The woman smiled, too, and the look that passed between them spoke of the things they shared, the attitudes and lessons of their years. They were of the same age, just as Pio and Louise were. "Men are easily fooled," Maria agreed, but I think you less so than most."

Slocum nodded and Maria looked toward the house again. "I can't say I would have chosen a whore," she said bluntly. "But who can tell where our lives will take us? I have a good feeling about that one." She turned back. "Just as I had about you, Mr. Slocum."

"Me?"

"I knew you did not belong with the judge. And I knew you would come to realize it"

"It took a while."

Maria Jameson laid a hand on Slocum's arm. "But you are here now, when it would have been easier to run, and I am more grateful than you can know. Will you stay here with us a while?"

The warm hand on his arm, the lack of sleep, the thrust of the woman's breasts beneath her white blouse, and the wild hope in his mind were all too much for Slocum. His head swam and his body began to sway. Maria tightened her grip and supported his body against hers.

"How terrible of me to keep you out in the sun," she said. "Let's go inside."

14

Slocum was thinking about the rest of the day at Rancho Cabrillo as he set out early the next morning with Pio and Louise. Pio was driving the family surrey. Louise sat beside him and Slocum was alone in back. They started early to take advantage of the cool morning air, equipped with long linen dusters to protect the fancy clothes they wore, also courtesy of the ranch. They were on their way to meet with the Jameson family's attorney, who had his office in Pasadena.

"He will be able to take the deposition," Maria Jameson had said the night before. "And he can tell us how to proceed."

Maria had told Louise that she would be a welcome guest at the ranch as long as she wished to stay and enjoy its protection. Louise had exchanged looks first with Pio, who tried to hide his excitement, and then with Slocum. For Slocum she had an expression that was hopeful and troubled at the same time. He smiled and nodded his head in encouragement, but later she was still looking concerned when she found the chance to talk with him alone.

"You realize it wasn't just business with us?" she said.

"I understand," Slocum assured her.

"I like you a lot..."

"But there's something special about Pio," he finished. "That's just the way it works sometimes, and that's the way it should be. I'm glad for you, Louise. For Pio, too. It might mean a future for both of you. And, hell, I'm just an old-timer who'll never settle down anyway."

Louise had laughed and kissed his cheek, her eyes gleaming with tears. "You ain't no old-timer," she whispered in his ear. "I bet there'll be nights when I wish you could teach him a few more tricks besides how to shoot."

"He's a fast learner," Slocum had said with a grin that suddenly turned serious. "But thanks just the same, Louise. I'll be thinking of you on those same nights."

Now, however, with Louise directly in front of him in the surrey, Slocum was remembering the way Maria Jameson had made them feel comfortable in her home. There had been hot baths immediately, with fresh clothes waiting for them when they got out. There had been a small feast prepared at noon, followed by a long afternoon's siesta in the best beds in the house. And in the evening, after a light supper, there had been an impromptu fandango that filled the house with music and laughter, much of it Maria's own. Slocum had danced with the woman several times, holding her in his arms and always reluctant to let her go. Her capacity for fun seemed as great as her strength and spirit. His admiration for her grew by the moment. He admired the warmth of her home and her hospitality, the quality of her management of the ranch, and the quality of her son. She was a rare woman, and she produced in Slocum a rare feeling that was far more than simple lust.

The feeling terrified him. But, as he bounced along in the surrey, distractedly watching the orange groves and then the cattle ambling through the sage and greasewood, he realized that the fear was simply an old instinct. Nearly all his life he had fought clear of anything that threatened to tie him down to one place or one person. That instinct made a lot less sense now that he was getting older and his bones were getting more brittle. The call of new places and new experiences was slowly losing its power—especially compared to the life he could imagine living with someone like Maria Jameson beside him. Slocum stirred restlessly at the thought of her, wondering if fate could have been planning this all along, bringing together these two people at just the right time. Why had Slocum felt the urge to come to Los

Angeles in the first place? He was just superstitious enough to think that it might have been more than chance.

The desert road took them along the rim of Arroyo Seco for a mile or so before it swung east onto Colorado Boulevard, where they were quickly caught up in a jumble of other wagons and buckboards clogging the wide, dusty street.

"I think the traffic gets worse every day," Pio said. "It's been unbearable since May, when the Santa Fe came to town."

Slocum saw land offices everywhere he looked, with people in all kinds of costumes streaming in and out. Some looked tense, as if they had their minds set on beating everyone else to the choicest lots, while others looked bewildered by the rush and confusion. Livery stables were renting out carriages and horses almost as fast as they could be got ready, and Pio had to watch out for the unexpected twists and turns of the drivers unfamiliar with their rigs. He managed to arrive safely at the intersection with Fair Oaks Avenue, where he pulled in close to the boardwalk and watered his horses at a stone trough provided by the Reid & Hummell Development Company. Their name was painted on a small wooden sign mounted above the trough. Slocum shook his head and followed Pio and Louise to the attorney's office.

He sensed something wrong almost as soon as they opened the door.

"Well, if it isn't Pio Jameson!" boomed the lawyer. His name was Wade Franklin, and he looked more like a country doctor than a lawyer. He weighed at least two hundred and fifty pounds, quite a few of which he carried in the heavy jowls of his face. His small eyes had a merry twinkle behind their wire-rimmed glasses, but after a while Slocum decided the twinkle was merely a professional affectation. There was no warmth in it at all, particularly when Franklin looked beyond Pio Jameson at Slocum and Louise.

Pio handed the lawyer an envelope and said, "A pleasure, sir. This is an authorization from my mother, confirming that I'm here on family business. I'd like to present Miss Louise Spring and Mr. John Slocum."

Slocum shook the lawyer's thick, fleshy hand, surprised to realize it was the first time he had heard the girl's last name.

Franklin ushered them to an inner office and closed the door with grave formality, indicating their seats as he lowered himself on the other side of a spacious mahogany desk. Slocum noticed a telephone box on one corner, and wondered if the contraptions would wind up in every home and store some day. Franklin was tilting Pio's envelope to catch the light streaming in through the open window over his shoulder. "You'll excuse me a moment," he said, the cold twinkle still in his eyes. Then he tore open the envelope and almost jumped back when a sheaf of bills fell to the top of his desk.

"I should have mentioned," Pio said stiffly. "My mother felt there would be a concern on your part that your services would go unrewarded."

"Not at all," said Franklin, a little too breezily. He read the short note, frowning, then absently picked up the paper money and formed it into a stack on his desk while he once again studied Slocum and Louise. "Your mother says this woman has evidence we could use in a bankruptcy hearing?"

"That's correct," said Pio. "She was being paid to spread a rumor that our bank was poorly managed." He told the lawyer the whole story, including the attempt on Slocum's life and their suspicion Judge Boyer was behind it all.

"I see," Franklin said thoughtfully. He drummed his fingers on the little stack of bills and turned to Louise. "May I ask you to tell the story in your own way?"

"Yes, sir!" The words caught in the girl's throat, so she repeated them.

Franklin smiled in a way that made Slocum's stomach tighten. It was meant to be reassuring. "Just relax, Miss Spring. You're among friends here. Let's begin with how you broadcast the information. Was it simply a casual thing, or did you have some employment at the time?"

Louise lowered her eyes. "Yes, sir," she said again, almost whispering. "I was a . . . I was working at the Rialto, in Los Angeles."

A rigid line of muscle showed along Pio's jaw. Franklin nodded slowly, as he might before the witness stand. Slocum could almost smell the courtroom around them.

"I'm sorry, Miss Spring, but I must ask. That is a brothel, is it not?"

Louise nodded.

"And was it there that you told . . . uh . . . other people about the alleged difficulties at the Church and Jameson Bank?"

Again the girl nodded.

"You were paid for doing so?"

"It wasn't so much," Louise said softly. "Just a slightly higher percentage of . . . my earnings."

"And who, precisely, paid you?"

"It was the piano player, Mark Weber. He liked to sit at the piano there, so people wouldn't notice him so much—it was sort of a disguise—but he was also the one in charge of everything that happened. He was the one who told me what to do."

"Was he the only one?"

"Yes, sir."

"Did he tell you why?"

"He just said it was part of some business deal."

"Did he tell you where *his* orders came from?" the lawyer asked.

Louise shook her head helplessly. "I don't think he ever said anything about that."

Franklin leaned forward "Did he ever even hint that there *was* someone giving him orders?"

The girl frowned thoughtfully. "Well, I just assumed . . . I mean, when he talked about a business deal . . ."

"But he never actually said, 'I've been told to spread these rumors,' or anything like that?"

"No, sir, he just told me what to tell my . . . what to say. When I asked why, he said it was a business deal, and that's all."

"And you just went along with it?" the lawyer sneered.

The girl flashed him a look. "You don't know Mark Weber," she said. "He likes to hurt people. I didn't want to give him any excuses."

Franklin sighed suddenly and leaned back in his chair, shaking his head "There you are," he said to Pio. "It's hopeless."

"What do you mean?"

"The girl's story isn't worth anything. What does it prove?"

Pio couldn't believe what he was hearing. "It's fraud!" he said. "Boyer can't get away with it!"

"Now, wait," said the lawyer. "It's only fraud if you can prove that the judge had anything to do with the rumors."

"But he's the only one who'd have any reason," protested the boy.

"Perhaps," said the lawyer, not quite meeting Pio's eye. "But guesswork isn't evidence."

"What about the whole picture?" Pio began. "What about Weber's attempt on Slocum's life?"

Franklin shrugged. "Again, who's to say he wasn't acting on his own?"

"He had a key," Slocum said softly.

Franklin sat up, looking more alert. "Weber had a key?"

"That's right. But the night clerk didn't give it to him. At least he says he didn't, and I believe him. The night clerk *did* give a copy to the judge. I think he'd swear to it in court. Is that enough of a connection?"

Franklin was frowning down at the top of his desk, one finger still tapping the bundle of bills.

"There's also the way Boyer disappeared when he saw me coming out that door," said Slocum. "Not hard evidence, I suppose, but it's suggestive."

"Damn it," said Pio, coming alive again, "even if you

can't do anything with Miss Spring's testimony by itself, you could at least start an investigation. Isn't it enough to get Mark Weber on the witness stand? You might even get the sheriff to take him in for questioning."

The lawyer glanced at Pio, and looked down just as fast. "All on the word of a prostitute?" he said gruffly, shaking his head. "I'm sorry, son, but it just wouldn't work."

"It's our only chance!" said Pio. "What kind of lawyer are you that you won't use the only weapon we have to keep our ranch?"

Franklin drew himself up behind the desk. "A lawyer who gives advice based on his experience and training," he said with dignity. "My advice is that this would be a waste of time."

"But—" Pio began.

"If, in your *wisdom,* you disagree, then perhaps you would like to retain other counsel."

"That's exactly what I'd like to do," Pio said. He stood suddenly and scooped the stack of bills from the lawyer's desk. "I may be wet behind the ears, Mr. Franklin, but I haven't yet learned how to sit behind a big desk and give up a fight before I even get started."

The lawyer tried for a cold stare, but his eyes still didn't quite meet Pio's. He shrugged and dipped his head in silent acquiescence.

There was no more to say. Pio turned on his heel and marched from the office, Louise and Slocum close behind. It was a grand exit. Slocum enjoyed his part in it. But Pio hesitated once they were outside, not sure what to do next.

Slocum gripped his arm and said, "Good job, boy! But we're not through with him yet. This way."

His hand still on Pio's arm, Slocum guided the boy hurriedly around the corner and into the alley that paralleled Colorado Boulevard. Louise followed, looking puzzled. Slocum held a finger to his lips and began to move more carefully. In a moment they heard the lawyer's muffled voice, drifting out through the open window of his office. They crept closer.

"...all three of them," Franklin was saying into his telephone. "That's right, they just left....I don't know, maybe here in town. They hadn't traveled far....No, I simply told them there was nothing in the girl's testimony to implicate you. I can't say whether they believed it or not. The boy stormed out of here in a huff, but he may calm down....I think that Slocum is the one to worry about. He looked like a tough hombre, and he was putting the pieces together pretty well in here....Well, thank you very much, Your Honor. That's more than generous....yes, I'll be looking for it in the mail. Do you expect any change in status?...That soon?...Good! I think we can look forward to a long and prosperous association."

As Franklin hung up the telephone, Slocum saw that the girl's eyes were wide with astonishment. Pio was trembling with fury. Slocum put his finger to his lips again and all three of them backed quietly out of the alley. On Fair Oaks they began walking rapidly, circling the block the long way so they could return to the surrey without passing Franklin's office door.

"How did you know?" Pio demanded as they walked.

"I smelled it," said Slocum.

"Smelled what?"

"I don't know. Maybe something about the way he couldn't look you in the eye. But the thing that really made me sure was when he told you to give it all up."

"Why?"

Slocum opened his mouth, then changed his mind. "You tell me," he said. "It's an exercise in human nature, and the kind of thinking you have to do sometimes to survive."

"Human nature," Pio mused aloud.

"Well," said Slocum with a wry smile, "a lawyer's nature, anyway. A lot of people would say there's a difference."

Pio's face brightened immediately. "Of course!" he said. "What kind of lawyer would turn down a good court fight—"

"—when there's even the remotest possible chance of success—"

"—which gives him the slightest excuse to rake in a fee. You're right, Slocum. No lawyer turns down a chance to earn a fee."

Slocum grinned at the boy. "You're learning fast," he said with pride. "So what do we do now?"

"Try to find another lawyer?"

Slocum nodded. "And fast, before Boyer has a chance to get reinforcements up here after us."

15

"Not one of those bastards wanted the case," Pio told his mother that night at dinner. He was rebuked with a sharp look and said "I'm sorry, but that's still too soft a word for those—"

"Pio! You may be absolutely right in your opinion, son, but we still have manners to observe at the dinner table."

"Yes, Mother."

The boy was careful not to look at Louise or Slocum—it was the only way for him to preserve his dignity—but Slocum saw that Louise was watching Pio with affection. Suddenly she winked at Slocum, and he realized that in many ways she was older and wiser than Pio. *Maybe that's the way it is,* Slocum thought. *Women seem to understand some parts of life long before men do.*

"Did you truly visit every attorney in Pasadena?" Maria Jameson asked her son. She used a businesslike tone, as between equal partners, and Slocum felt that confirmed what he'd just been thinking.

"Not by a long shot!" Pio said fervently. "I never would have believed how many lawyers one town can support. But after a while Mr. Slocum thought it was a good idea for us to leave."

Maria looked puzzled for a moment, then said, "Because of the telephone call, Mr. Slocum?"

He nodded, swallowing a piece of tender steak. "If Judge Boyer had a few men on hand with a few fast horses," Slocum said, "he might have tried to cut us off from Los Angeles. There was even the possibility that he had some contacts in Pasadena, who could have been looking for us even then. He'd only need one telephone call." Slocum shook his head sadly. "Those machines sure have changed things a lot." What he didn't say was that they were more or less the reason he'd been trying to stay on the right side of the law for the last few years. Telephone and telegraph wires were being strung everywhere alongside the highways, and railroad lines that were spreading just as fast. They were like the strands of a huge net that could be drawn together in a few hours' time. And whatever could work for the law could also work for some people outside the law.

"Is it possible we are giving the man too much credit?" Maria Jameson asked. "Can he really be that dangerous?"

"He's been one step ahead of us so far," Slocum said with a shrug. "I'd say he knows his way around the chessboard."

"I don't understand how he even knew Mr. Franklin was our attorney."

"Don't forget that he's a judge. It would be a matter of record who appears for you."

"But to buy up all the lawyers in Pasadena!"

Slocum coughed politely. "I'm not so sure he did, Mrs. Jameson. The other attorneys seemed more frightened than anything. I suspect word has gotten 'round that bad things might happen to people who stand in his way."

"All the more reason that someone should, Mr. Slocum."

Slocum smiled with pleasure at the woman's spirit and said, "I'm not disagreeing. But so far the people who stood in his way haven't come out very well. Why should anyone try to play the hero, especially when there isn't very much to gain and everything to lose?"

"You're right, of course. We seem to have a shortage of heroes these days." Her dark, unreadable eyes lingered on Slocum for a long minute, making him uncomfortable. He was glad when she finally turned to Pio. "What shall we do now, son?"

The boy glanced uncertainly at Slocum. "Could we find this Mark Weber, this piano player, and try to make him tell us who paid him?"

"Even if we got to him without stumbling over Boyer's men," Slocum said, "and even if we could make him talk, how could we make him repeat the story to a judge?"

"Pay him, perhaps?"

Slocum shook his head. "He'd probably double-cross you, Pio. He might even tell the judge we tried to bribe him, which would make everything worse."

"Why would he do that?"

"Profit, Pio. Pure and simple profit. That way he could take your money and Boyer's too. Besides, he'd figure that Boyer would have other jobs for him in the future. He'd want to to stay on the winning side."

Pio nodded slowly, letting the lesson sink in even though the knowledge made him sad. Suddenly his face turned angry. "There must be a way to fight that man!" he said. "Mother, do we have any friends in the governor's office? Could we ask for an investigation of some kind?"

"I have had similar thoughts," said Maria. "There is an old clerk in Sacramento who was friendly to your grandfather. I don't know whether he has any influence with the governor, but perhaps, now that we have the story of Miss Spring . . ."

"It would have been better to have the affidavit," Slocum said, "but it wouldn't hurt to try. It might be that the governor has heard some other rumblings about Marcus Boyer. This would give him an excuse to do something."

"If you will draft a letter," Pio told his mother decisively, "I will send one of our men with it in the morning."

"Of course."

"We must also consider the bankruptcy hearing," Pio said thoughtfully. He looked at Louise with a mixture of hope and regret. "It appears the bank will run out of money very soon," he explained. "When the doors close for good there will be a court hearing in Los Angeles, where the judge can present his claims. That is where we had hoped to use your sworn statement."

Pio faltered and Louise said, "Are you asking me to testify in person?"

"It could be dangerous," the boy said in anguished tones. "It could also be . . . painful to you. Painful and embarrassing."

"But it might help?"

"Even that is not certain. But if the hearing officer is fair . . ."

There was a strained silence at the table while Louise frowned at her plate. "We wouldn't ask you to do it without reward," Maria began, but Louise shook her head impatiently and the older woman stopped talking. When Louise looked up again her eyes were shining with tears.

"It's *my* fault that this is happening," she said.

Both Jamesons started to protest, mother and son, but again the girl cut them off. "The other banks survived the scare, didn't they? Who's to say your bank wouldn't have done just as well if it weren't for those things I said? If you lose the ranch it'll be partly my doing. Of *course* I want the chance to make it right!"

And if we win," Maria said softly, "it will be thanks to your courage."

"It isn't courage," Louise said, "it's guilt!" She sniffled, then laughed nervously. "Guilt's a lot worse than fear."

The others laughed, too, and Slocum said "Amen to that!" They were silent a moment, unsure what to say next, until Maria announced gravely that there was something more to consider.

"You may as well all hear this," she began. "A man came this morning from the Farmers and Merchants Assurance Corporation. It seems Will Church had a life policy with them. He increased the amount, and changed the policy to make me the beneficiary, just a couple of days before he died."

She was looking directly at Slocum as she said the last

few words, and the impact on him was like the lifting of a great weight. "I'll be damned," he roared. Then, "I'm sorry, ma'am, but the thing has sorely troubled me."

"Of course," she said. "You were angry that he forced your hand?"

Slocum nodded. "I knew he was committing suicide—he kept saying he couldn't live with himself after what he'd gotten you into—but I thought he was just using me to do the dirty work. Thank you for telling me, ma'am."

"I have the feeling I'm missing something," Louise said timidly.

"The company may not have had to pay out on the policy," said Maria, "if Mr. Church had died by his own hand."

"He was using me after all," Slocum finished, "but not because he didn't have the guts to do it himself. He was making sure that Mrs. Jameson and her son would have a little something left."

"In the end, his heart was in the right place," Maria agreed. "And it was no small gesture. The insurance man left a check for forty-five thousand dollars."

Slocum raised an eyebrow. Pio whistled softly.

"The question we face now," said Maria, "is how to use the money."

"It would keep the bank open only a few more days," Pio said thoughtfully. "Unless we waited to use it until *after* we exposed Marcus Boyer. Then, perhaps, if confidence was restored . . ."

"That is the problem," said the boy's mother. "It is still a gamble. The insurance money, with our savings, could also be used to buy another small farm or ranch." Pio started to protest, but she held up her hand. "I know it wouldn't go far in California," she said with a smile. "It would barely buy us two lots on the ocean. But elsewhere—in Oregon, perhaps—it could mean a new beginning for us."

"This is our home," Pio said hotly. "I never believed I'd see the day when you would give up the place where our people are buried."

Maria smiled approvingly at her son. "I merely suggest alternatives for you to consider," she said. "I want to fight as much as you do, but I also have known hardship, where you have not. To gamble everything we have, and lose . . ." Maria Jameson shook her head. "You cannot know what it would be like to start with nothing, my son."

"We won't lose!"

The woman nodded slowly. "I have heard those words before," she said softly. "Many of my father's friends were sure the Americans would honor the Mexican land grants, as they promised. But life is not always just, Pio."

"Perhaps not, but the judge will certainly not win. I have vowed that Marcus Boyer will never live to own our ranch, and I repeat it now."

"Son . . ." Maria began. She opened her mouth, but there were no words. She looked helplessly at Slocum.

"I'll repeat myself as well," Slocum said harshly. "Killing a man solves nothing. It is the absolute worst thing you could do. Especially when there is still the hope of another strategy."

The boy stared at him defiantly.

"I'm warning you," Slocum added. "If you try anything you'll have me to answer to."

Some of the defiance disappeared, and Maria gave Slocum a grateful look. Once again her eyes lingered on his, full of some deep feeling he couldn't understand. "I am still concerned about the judge," she said after a while, speaking to her son. "If he has so much power, do you think he would try to come here in his search for Slocum and Louise?"

"I don't believe even he would be so bold," Pio said doubtfully.

"If I may . . ." Slocum offered. "I've had a chance to know the man better than most. I believe he is unbalanced and unpredictable."

Pio's frown was troubled. "It might be wise to post lookouts in the morning, and keep some horses near at hand in the corral. In fact"—He pushed away from the table.—"if you'll excuse me I'll go out to the horse pasture now, before it is fully dark."

Louise took the linen napkin from her lap and placed it on the table with a flourish, asking if she could join Pio in his chore. He nodded, and the two of them left the room. They didn't see the knowing grin that passed between Slocum and Maria.

"Are you jealous of my son?" Maria asked with a smile.

"Yes, ma'am," said Slocum, meeting her gaze. "I think he's very lucky to have you for his mother."

The woman started to laugh, then stopped when she saw that Slocum wasn't smiling. She put a hand to her throat and surprised him with a sad, longing look. "I have tried," she said, "but it has been very hard. And there are some things a mother cannot do, ever. Would you like to walk with me, Mr. Slocum?"

16

"I have very much enjoyed your company these past two evenings," said Maria Jameson.

They were her first words in the ten minutes or so since they'd left the house. They sounded like a preamble, which wasn't surprising, since the woman had clearly been studying on something in her silence. Slocum had occasionally given her a sidelong glance as they strolled over the desert in the twilight, but otherwise he had let her think in peace. Now, standing beneath an orange tree, he smiled and said, "Is it because I'm such a fine dancer?"

Maria smiled and said no, then corrected herself. "I'm sure that's part of it, Mr. Slocum. You are a man who is not afraid to laugh, who knows how to have a good time."

"I can thank my hostess for all of that."

"Ah. Then there is your impeccable grace and manner," the women said with another smile. "You are a true gentleman."

"That's very kind," said Slocum, genuinely pleased.

"But you are so much more!" Maria said feelingly. "You are truly a *man*, and that is what I have missed in these empty years."

"I'm surprised," Slocum said modestly. "I should think eligible men would be swarming around a woman of your beauty—"

"A woman of my property, you mean." The bitter words were tinged with scorn. "They come sniffing around, yes, but the hunger in their eyes is not for me. It is for Rancho Cabrillo."

"I can't believe that's true of all of them."

Maria dismissed them with a wave of her hand. "It doesn't matter. They are all the same. They are small. They are not men, like my father was a man . . . like you are." She looked up into Slocum's eyes and it seemed that there was a flush in her cheeks although it might have been the deepening gloom of dusk. "You remind me so much of him! You see clearly what is true and what is false, and are not afraid to go where your thoughts lead you. You are hard and strong, and also kind." Maria's chest was rising and falling with labored breathing. "In short, John Slocum, you seem to be everything I would want my son to be. And"—She dropped her gaze, finishing in little more than a whisper—"and everything I have wanted for myself."

Slocum put his arms around her and said, "You've been very lonely, haven't you?"

"It's been hard," she said into his chest. Then suddenly she was pulling away from him. "I hate people who complain," she snapped. "That was not my intention." Slocum chuckled, and she demanded to know why.

"Was your father also stubborn?" he said. "I wonder if you aren't a little like him yourself."

"It's possible," she said, and laughed. "It's more than possible."

"He would have been proud of you."

"Thank you," Maria said absently. She was studying Slocum, apparently not finished with what she had to say. "I tell you all of this for a reason," she finally continued. "Not for sympathy, but so you understand my . . . idea."

"I'm still listening."

"I would not be talking like this if the next few days weren't so uncertain, but who knows when you might be forced to leave—or want to." Slocum started to protest, but the woman cut him off. "I am offering you a partnership, Mr. Slocum, so that this fight will truly be your fight as well."

"A partnership?"

"A home," said Maria. "I want you to stay with us—with me. I don't know how it will be, but there is no time to find out, or for me to use a woman's tricks and charms. Therefore, I want you to know that there is a place for you with us, whether as a friend and partner, or . . ." She gave him a direct look and said, "Do you truly think I am beautiful?"

"Uncommonly," said Slocum. He brushed her cheek with his fingers and tried to find words. "I could not forget the sight of you," he began, before he realized that words weren't necessary. He bent to kiss her upturned lips, and shivered even though the night air was warm. Her mouth yielded to his and responded with hunger as she pressed her body close under the pressure of his arms. He felt the heat of her firm, heavy breasts, but for the moment all he could think about was kissing her.

He was so surprised that he stopped a moment to stare down at her lovely face and her dark, haunting eyes, unable to remember another time in his life when he had been so powerfully affected by only a kiss. No other lips had ever tasted so sweet.

Slocum kissed her again and let his hand roam down her back and below her waist, cupping and caressing the roundness of her thighs and buttocks. Her tongue began to explore his mouth, hot and darting, while her body squirmed against his, rubbing everywhere. His hands were moving wildly, desperately trying to touch everything at once, as if they could never get enough. He began to unbutton the white blouse and her hands flew up, not to stop him but to help him. He shivered again. When her breasts were hanging free Maria pulled Slocum's shirt wide and brushed her nipples through the hair on his chest, then crushed herself against him once again. Her thighs arched forward, pressing the small of her belly against the bulge in Slocum's pants. Her hands squeezed the hard muscle of Slocum's broad shoulders, then dropped down to work on his belt and the zipper in the store-bought trousers he wore. In an instant his cock was free, tingling with the feel of the desert breeze and the hungry stroking of the woman's hands.

He took Maria's breasts in his own hands and hefted them, kneading them gently as he watched the shift of their weight. He rolled her nipples between his fingers, and was rewarded when she threw her head back, groaning toward the sky. She began fumbling with her skirt and the ruffled things beneath it, wriggling free of them and letting them fall. She stood first on one foot and then the other to kick them aside, then wrapped her arms around Slocum's neck and pressed herself forward once again, gently, so that Slocum's cock was caressed by the soft flesh of her belly while she sought his mouth with a wonderful greed.

"We can't," said Slocum. "Your clothes . . . the dirt . . ."

"I don't care! I want you here under the stars."

"I have a better idea," Slocum breathed. He cupped his hands beneath her and lifted her without strain. She gasped, holding onto his neck with one arm while she used the other hand to guide him in. He slipped inside, instantly soaking, feeling her legs lock behind him. With a powerful grip he lifted her again and lowered her, lifted and lowered, almost withdrawing and then plunging himself to the hilt. Maria hugged his head to her breasts, gripping his shoulders and feeling the play of his corded muscles as he lifted and lowered, lifted and lowered.

"So strong," Maria cried. She shuddered, and her legs gripped him tighter. "Oh, Lord, so strong!" The words caught in her throat and she began to moan as he continued thrusting himself as deep as he could go. He quickened the pace, feeling her ready, and she cried out to him to go even faster. She leaned back so that she could bend down to find his mouth with hers, sucking at his lips while their bodies moved together in a frenzy, her breasts bobbing against his chest. Suddenly her lips slackened and she pulled away, arching her back, her arms and legs locked about him in a death grip. Her face was thrown to the sky, her mouth wide open, but there was no sound for a moment. Then there came a strangled whimper, but Slocum was lost in the rush of fever through his body and the lightness in his head as he released himself inside her. He was plunging wildly upward, hungry for the last possible sensation before it began subsiding into a warm afterglow.

When his head cleared, he felt strong and clear and fresh. This, too, was different from the vaguely sad emptiness that often lingered after he had been with other women. The night air felt good on his body, as good as Maria's loving hands. He sank slowly to his knees, without withdrawing, leaning back on his haunches so that Maria could sit on his lap. They stayed together for several long, sweet moments, holding each other, kissing softly.

"I was not made to be denied this," Maria whispered in his ear. "It has been too long."

Slocum understood that this was part of the woman's proposition, and the thought made him giddy. He realized he was being offered everything he thought he'd lost more than twenty years before: a woman such as he'd never dreamed existed, a piece of fine land to work, and a fine young man to take it over when the time was right. He would eat well by day, rest his head on the same pillow every night. He would become known, perhaps respected. He would live out his days among friends.

"It may be that my wandering days are through," Slocum murmured.

Maria squeezed him in her arms and kissed his ear. "I would work to see that you never regret it," she said with feeling. "And sometimes, perhaps in spring, when you get the faraway look in your eye . . ."

"I could take trips, maybe visit a few old haunts."

"I would not try to tie you to me, John Slocum. You are too much of a man for that."

Slocum closed his eyes and took a deep breath. "I'll think on it," he told her. "I make no promises. It's not easy to break the habits of a lifetime."

"I understand. I'll say no more, except to ask, a man

cannot be without a home forever, can he? Till the end of his days?"

"I don't imagine," Slocum said. "I've thought on that very subject, but sometimes it seemed that I would never find the place for me."

Maria kissed his ear again, her warm breath seeming to reach across his tingling flesh. "I hope you have," she whispered. "And what is that I feel getting so hard again? Shall we go inside now, where we can see each other and enjoy the comfort of a soft bed?" Maria giggled like a small girl, showing Slocum yet another side of her personality. "We have the whole night together," she said, "and I am getting some very wicked ideas."

17

Slocum snapped awake to the sound of fists pounding on a door. When he opened his eyes, the pounding had stopped. He found Maria in his arms, staring at him with wide eyes. Through the window that opened on the courtyard there was only the suggestion of a dim grey sky. He almost could imagine that the noise had been part of a dream.

Then it came again: the loud hammering of fists. This time there was also a voice. "Open up, Mrs. Jameson. It's Judge Boyer."

Maria leaped from the bed, grabbing for the skirt and blouse she had worn the night before. Slocum glanced at the store-bought slacks and said, "Where's the pants I came in?" Maria stopped dressing long enough to find them in a chest of drawers.

"Come on out," Boyer yelled from outside. "I'm seizing your ranch 'til the hearing. The bank closed its doors for good last night."

"The bastard!" Maria cried. She ran from the room, still fumbling with her buttons, Slocum right behind her. They ran down the hall to the common living area, next to the kitchen, where Pio Jameson was already staring at the big oak door with black hatred in his eyes and the Smith and Wesson levelled in his hands.

"Give it up," Boyer yelled again, a few feet away. "I got a writ that says it's legal, and I got ten men around the house. There's nowhere to go."

Louise stumbled into the room, dressed in her riding clothes. All four looked at each other for a moment, frozen, until Slocum said, "Is there any way out of here?"

"Can you risk it?" Maria whispered.

"We're dead if we stay."

The woman looked at her son. "Over the roof?" When he nodded, Maria turned to Slocum. "Pio will go with you."

"But Mother—"

"No!" said Slocum.

"You do not—"

"Open up" screamed the judge. "Aren't you in there, Pierce? Unlock this door or I'll smash it down!"

"Give us a moment," called Maria, and then in a grim tone said to Slocum, "You do not know this country. They will track you down in an hour, if you even manage to get away by yourself." Slocum opened his mouth, but Maria pushed him away. "There is no time for foolishness. He also gets away to fight with better advantage. Don't you see?"

"But you'll be alone," said the boy.

"Some of the *vaqueros* will stay. I'll be fine. Now *go!*"

She advanced on them, herding them reluctantly toward the courtyard. It was a haven in the center of the house, protected on all four sides by the thick adobe of the outer walls. Hastily they gathered provisions and checked their weapons by the light of a coal-oil lamp. Without it they could see only vague shapes in the pre-dawn darkness. Boyer was yelling again, hammering on the door. Then the hammering got heavier, as if Boyer's men had brought up a battering ram. The pounding became slow and insistent, shaking the house, and the three would-be travelers speeded their preparations.

Maria Jameson was dragging a ladder from against one wall, upending it between two vegas protruding from the adobe. Slocum noticed a rain gutter opening and asked if there was a wall around the roof.

"About two feet only," she said, and pointed beyond the ladder. "The corral is in that direction."

"I loose-saddled the horses last night," Pio said. "Just in

case. They'll only need a few tugs on the cinch."

"Good!" said Slocum. "Wait here." He climbed the ladder and disappeared for a moment, then came back down. "There's at least three of 'em out back," he said in a low voice. "Pio, are you up to tightening those cinches and opening the gate while I keep you covered from the roof?"

The boy swallowed hard and nodded.

"Then let's go," Slocum said. He followed the boy up the ladder and watched Louise come behind him. He had one last sight of Maria Jameson handing up their gear, which they dragged across the roof as they crawled toward the outside wall. There Slocum lay down his Winchester long enough to rummage in his bag for the spare Colt and a box of .44-40's. A small handful of the thick, stubby shells went into his shirt pocket, with the flap buttoned down. They'd fit both his Winchester and his Colts, but they were for later. Right now, between all three guns, he had just twenty-five rounds to pin down at least three men, probably more. He couldn't afford to stop shooting for more than a second or two, or the judge's men would get wise and spend more time on their aim, and it would be Pio who'd be out in the open.

"You better work fast," Slocum whispered to Pio. "I'd hate to use up everything I got here. I figure you've got about thirty seconds."

"I can do it, Slocum."

"I'm sure you can, son, but keep an eye peeled just the same. Louise, you'll be throwing the bags down, and then you go get that ladder for yourself."

"I can jump," she murmured.

"It's a long way down."

"Yeah, but it's *faster*."

Slocum chuckled and said, "Suit yourself. Everyone ready?"

At Pio's nod, Slocum popped above the roofline and snapped off a shot at the nearest gunman he had seen, a shadowy figure posted at the far edge of the corral. The figure ducked and Pio slipped over the edge, landing with a dull thump on the earth below. Louise began tossing their bags down behind him.

"Keep down!" Slocum hissed, jumping to the right and firing again just as the figure by the corral started to straighten up. The man apparently realized how badly he was exposed. With a quick shot over his shoulder he raced farther into the desert for the protection of a rock that gleamed softly in the pale light.

As the gunfighter ran Slocum was jumping again, this time to the left, into the corner of the roof above the corral. He looked straight down on a man with a Winchester who was drawing a bead on Pio. There was no time for fancy shooting. Slocum fired down in to the man's body and watched him fall, the Winchester exploding harmlessly into the dirt. Slocum cursed bitterly, knowing there'd be hell to pay for any killing. There was a blast from behind even as he was ducking away. A slug whistled over his head. Someone was running around from the front of the building. But there was also the man off behind the bunkhouse, whom he still hadn't reckoned with. He fired in that direction first, dusting the man back behind the corner, then aimed down at the sound of the man running through the shadows next to the wall. He heard a yelp above the roar of his Colt and, he hoped, the sound of the man retreating back toward the front. He wasn't sure of anything now. His ears were ringing painfully from the explosions and he knew he'd have to go by sight from here on in.

He'd been counting his shots, and now he stuffed the empty Colt in his waistband, the loaded one still in its holster. With the carbine he got off two more shots, one each for the man behind the bunkhouse and the man behind the rock. He'd found each of them just as they were exposing themselves for better aim. The one behind the bunkhouse got off a round, but Slocum had spoiled his shot.

Louise threw over the last bag and cringed behind the low parapet. Slocum saw movement by the far corner of the house and swung his carbine for a quick shot, then swung back for two more at the rock and the bunkhouse. He was leaping to the side after every round, randomly to the left and right, and his legs were getting sore. But still he roamed from one side of the house to the other, firing down on anyone who tried to advance from the front. The smell of powder burned his nose and lungs and he became like a madman, possessed by remembered echoes of a war he'd fought so long ago it was like another lifetime. Once again it seemed that he was in Kansas, trapped in the old stone farmhouse with Quantrill, knowing that his only chance for escape lay in sheer desperate fury. The enemy would be afraid of crazy men. They would spook him. Slocum let loose with a blood-curdling Rebel yell and fired again at rock and bunkhouse.

Pio had their bags tied onto the saddles of the three horses, which were prancing skittishly beneath the gunfire. It made Slocum nervous just to look at them, but by their pale glow Slocum guessed them to be grullas, big and sturdy mouse-colored mounts like Pio's own. The boy had their reins in his hand, fighting them as he backed toward the gate. Slocum jumped to one side of the house and fired at a man peeking around the front corner. He let go at the rock and bunkhouse again, then ran for the other side of the house. Nothing coming. When he looked again Pio had the gate open and was mounted on his own horse, leading the others toward the wall. Louise was sprawled in the soft muck of the corral, just getting her hands and legs beneath her. Slocum's teeth appeared in a ferocious grin. He vaulted over the wall, dropping beside the trailing horse and jumping into the saddle even as he slid the rifle into its sheath.

"Take the lead!" Slocum yelled to Pio. "Head for open ground! Hug your pony's neck, and for God's sake, don't bunch up!" He let loose with another shrill cry as the horses lunged out of the corral and directly between the gunmen behind the rock and bunkhouse. Slocum unlimbered his Peacemaker and sent a bullet careening off the rock as they went by, then swung back in time to see a shadow separate itself from the bunkhouse. He fired and saw the shadow crumple. Slocum cursed again. He hadn't been aiming for a kill. He twisted in his saddle and saw the man at the rock get off a couple of futile shots, while others swarmed around the house behind him. Slocum saw a few more stabs of flame, the bullets harmless in the gloom at a hundred yards and gaining. There was the shout of a command drifting across the desert and the gunfighters running for their horses, and then there was nothing but the pounding of their own horses' hooves, the wind in their hair and the blood beating through their veins. Young Pio glanced back and whooped. Louise had a sickly grin on her face, but a grin all the same.

Slocum tucked his reins beneath his arm and unbuttoned the flap of his shirt pocket, withdrawing one fat shell at a time and sliding it into the breach of his Winchester. When the tube was full he levered a shell into the chamber and had room for one more. He became aware that Pio was slackening his pace and the horses were following suit.

"Damn it, Pio," he bellowed, "keep 'em moving!"

"But we've got a half-mile lead on fresh mounts!" Pio called. "Why blow our animals when the others have already come twenty miles?"

Slocum glanced back, just able to make out four riders under the dust cloud they were raising. The judge had said he had brought ten. If he was being truthful, then he'd left another four to guard the home place, not counting the two men Slocum put under. But the pursuers were coming at them full out.

"When they slow down, we slow down," Slocum ordered. "Don't ever give up an edge if you don't have to."

"Yes, sir," yelled Pio.

"Don't look so hangdog, boy! Some things you only learn when you do 'em, or get caught *not* doin' 'em. We don't know what's ahead, so let's give ourselves all the leeway we can."

The three horses picked up speed, their breathing coming

loud now. Their hooves beat the desert floor and their rigging flapped along their necks. Slocum slipped the Winchester back into its scabbard and went to work on his Colts, punching out the empty shells and thumbing fresh ones in their place. This time he left an empty chamber under the hammer, since he could get by with the firepower he already had, and the empty chambers were a hell of a lot safer in this kind of action.

When they topped a small rise Slocum scanned the country behind them for any sign of pursuit besides the four men directly behind them. He didn't see any. He angled his pony closer to Pio's and yelled, "So where are we going?"

"I wish to God I knew," the boy yelled back with a wild grin. "I was just about to ask you the same thing."

Pio Jameson was being modest, caught up in the exhilaration of escape and the old frontier tradition of understatement. Or at least, that one side of the tradition. There was also the tradition of bluff and braggadocio, as practiced by the likes of Jim Bridger or Wild Bill Hickock—dead for many years—or almost any half-drunk saddle bum entering a saloon with a wild litany of things either he could do or someone could not do to him. But in general the braggart was a spinner of tall tales about past events. When it came to predictions, the favorite approach was modesty, as in, "This chil' jes' might bring in a pelt 'r two," or, "I reckon I could hold my own if it came to a fight." The appeal of modesty, of course, is that it makes no serious claims you have to live up to. If you lose, well, you tried and that's all you said you'd do. On the other hand, you're an even bigger winner if you come out on top, because all the world loves a modest hero. They're a bit easier to bear.

In any case, Pio Jameson knew exactly where he was going. He and the *vaqueros* he worked with had searched for straying cows on every square foot of the San Gabriel foothills, sometimes venturing into the mountains themselves when they were moved by the spirit of exploration.

He led Slocum and Louise through a maze of arroyos, climbing steadily as the sun climbed through the sky on the other side of the peaks towering above them. The four horsemen behind them had long since slowed to a walk, as did the trio of fugitives, but the pursuers remained implacably on their trail. The hours slipped by and the sun burned down from high above them, but still the judge's men came on.

"Do you think they mean to track us down and kill us?" Pio asked when they crossed a rocky point, temporarily losing sight of the trackers.

"I suppose we have to assume that's their intent," Slocum said grimly.

"We're coming to a kind of ledge up here. Maybe a mile or two. We could lay for 'em and hit 'em before they ever knew what happened."

"Ambush?" Slocum shook his head. "We'd have to be pretty desperate, Pio. Right now we want to stay as law-abiding as we can be, so the judge doesn't have too much ammunition to use against us. Things that might seen right out here, might seem like pure and simple *survival*, look a whole lot different in a courtroom when everyone's well-fed and civilized."

There was no response. Slocum glanced over at the boy as they rode and saw that he was thinking. They'd covered maybe a hundred yards before Pio nodded and said, "I think I understand what you say, Slocum. As long as there is any hope, your way, we will be as innocent as children." He smiled boyishly, glancing over his shoulder, and the smile turned into a worried frown. "Perhaps it's my imagination," he said, "but those men seem a lot closer than they were before."

"I doubt it," Slocum said, following Pio's gaze. "How could they . . . Jesus Christ, I think you're right!"

"But they're still just walking, no different than we are."

"They are now," Slocum said, "but when we lose them in an arroyo or over a rise, they're putting the spurs to their ponies. We'll have to do the same thing."

"Oh, God," Louise murmured. The two men looked at her and she said, "My backside has had too much already. I don't know if I'll ever sit again."

Pio and Slocum looked at each other. "Were you planning on losing them up in the mountains?" Slocum asked.

Pio glanced up at the barren desert ridges above him. "I was thinking we'd try, but it wouldn't be easy. It's mostly sand and low brush, Slocum. No trees or rock. Mostly we'd be leaving tracks for them to find and having a hard time staying out of sight."

Slocum was also staring up into the mountains, the habits and instincts of a lifetime telling him to run for cover. But his rational mind was sending a different message. "Even supposin' we made it," Slocum mused aloud, "where would that leave us? High and dry, with no way of knowing what was happening."

Pio's black eyes gleamed with excitement. "It might even be that Marcus Boyer *wants* us there, out of the way!"

"Good Lord, I ain't been thinking straight," said Slocum. "I just assumed that the hearing he mentioned would be a few days off. But what if he pulled some strings and got it scheduled already? For all we know, that hearing could be going on this afternoon."

Pio's eyes left Slocum to stare off in the direction of the city, his body straining forward as if he yearned to set his horse running immediately in that direction, but then his gaze swung west toward the dust cloud and the four horsemen less than half a mile behind them. Finally he looked at Louise with a wolfish grin.

"Praise heaven for your sore ass," he said.

18

They tried to change course as gradually as possible, as if the contours of the land made it necessary. They had been traveling north and east, into the mountains, but after an hour or so they were headed almost directly south. In the bottoms of the arroyos they gigged the horses into speed, covering half a mile here and a quarter of a mile there. It was a hard thing for the horses and Slocum could see the sympathy in Pio's eyes, but there was no water in their path and no time to look for any. Slowly they put distance between themselves and the four gunmen riding behind them, who finally must have realized the intent of their quarry. The pursuers could be seen pushing their horses into a steady canter, not worried about concealing the chase. But their animals were nearly played out and couldn't close the distance.

It was also too late to cut the trio off from their obvious goal. Their path was already a straight line toward the city of Pasadena, and by now they were close enough that they were beginning to see the surveyors' stakes tied with colored ribbons. The little pieces of cloth fluttered in the breeze and made Slocum think of people's hopes and dreams for southern California.

"Look at this!" Pio said with disgust. "If Marcus Boyer has his way, Rancho Cabrillo will be covered with these little stakes."

"Don't trouble yourself," Louise said. "We will stop him."

The boy looked at her a long moment as they rode side

by side, then shook his head and turned away as if embarrassed to speak.

"You're a lucky man," Slocum said.

Pio glanced back, eyes ready to show defiance if Slocum were teasing him. When he saw that Slocum was not, his eyes flashed with gratitude and acknowledgement. "There are not many women such as she, are there, Slocum?"

"No, Pio, not many." He was aware of Louise watching him. "I'm glad you have the eyes to see."

Pio Jameson glanced over his shoulder again, but he was all business now, perhaps a bit self-important as he squinted at the four riders behind them. "We're keeping our lead, Slocum. I'd make it better than a mile."

"Every little bit helps," Slocum said. "But it still won't give us much time to disappear once we hit town."

"And how will we do that?" Louise asked. "Another magic act?"

Slocum laughed, remembering their escape from the Rialto. "Maybe one'll come to me. All I can think of so far is losing ourselves in traffic."

"What if they start running when we get closer?" Pio asked.

"That's exactly what they'll do. They can't afford to let us get too far ahead. Only we'll beat them to it."

"You mean running the horses before they do?"

"I don't like it any more than you do, Pio, but we can't give up our lead. It'll be a close shave as it is."

"They've had no water since this morning."

"We'll leave 'em someplace with water. But if those gents behind us are running flat out, and we're still only a mile ahead, we won't have more than two or three minutes to spare."

Pio rubbed his pony's neck and said, "You're right, of course, but I hate to have to do it."

"Maybe we won't," Slocum said.

He saw two startled faces before Pio and Louise followed the direction of his gaze down toward the city. They had just crested a long mound of earth and now they were seeing, for the first time, a large wagon trundling across the desert about two miles below them. It looked like an old freighter, but, like the wagon Slocum had seen three days before, its cargo was people. They lined the benches built along each of the sidewalls gawking at the country while they listened to a man who faced them from his seat beside the teamster.

Louise grinned at Slocum. "Now you've pulled a rabbit out of a hat."

"Some rabbit," Pio muttered. "Those skunks are everywhere." He looked at Slocum. "Do you really think Boyer's men would leave us alone if we had company?"

"They couldn't risk it," Slocum assured him. "Maybe twenty years ago, when things were wilder . . . but now they'd have five different kinds of law down their throats."

Pio had been listening. Now he focused over Slocum's shoulder, and his tone became more urgent. "Let's hope you're right," he said, "because here they come. I think they've seen the wagon."

"They're trying to cut us off," Slocum yelled. "Let's move!"

All three of them spurred their horses and the grullas jumped forward as willingly as any Appaloosa, their great chests heaving and their heavy legs kicking up the dust. Slocum had to admire those animals. The pursuers never had a chance to close the gap. Instead they backed off when Slocum and Louise and Pio hauled in on the reins about twenty feet downwind of the wagon, waiting for the pall of dust to drift away before walking the heaving ponies up along the freighter's iron-rimmed wheels. All faces were turned toward them, some eyes wide with excitement, but it was the salesman on the front seat who spoke first. He was about Slocum's age, with steel-grey curls of hair, and his tone was a little stiff. He didn't appreciate the interruption.

"Might there be anything we can do for you?" he asked.

Slocum opened his mouth to say something lame, something about wanting a little company on the ride back into town, but then he took a second look at the eager faces turned in his direction. He realized the dudes were seeing three hard-bitten, heavily armed riders covered with dust and burned red by sun and wind. Some of them were also casting curious glances toward the four horsemen up on the ridge paralleling the wagon. Slocum was feeling a lot of things at once: a little anger at the dudes' intrusion into the West, a sudden knowledge of what would get their attention, and a little desire for mischief. *What the hell,* he thought to himself.

"We're trying to escape from a band of murderers," he said dramatically.

There were a few gasps from the wagon. Pio's face came around, his mouth falling open in surprise. He started to protest, but Slocum spoke first.

"Those men up there are trying to kill us so they can steal this young man's ranch. But they won't try anything if we can ride with you kind folks."

"Good Lord," murmured one young woman, "this is the real Wild West!"

Louise put her hand to her mouth and turned away, her body shaking.

"Is the lady feeling ill?" said another customer, a middle-aged man with a paunch that stretched his woolen vest. "She can have my seat."

"That's very generous,"Slocum said. "Louise, the gentleman's offering you a *cushioned* seat in the wagon."

The girl cleared her throat and stared longingly at the bench as the customer started to rise. "Thank you," she said regretfully. "I couldn't . . ."

"Nonsense," said the man, jumping down from the wagon.

Louise didn't stir, and Slocum thought he understood. She'd been in the saddle half the day and now she was so sore she wasn't sure she could move, or at least move with any degree of grace. Pio was looking puzzled so Slocum sidled his horse close to the girl's and said, "Grab my neck." He was already slipping his arm around her waist. Suddenly he angled his body over sideways, pivoting her across his hips, out of the saddle, and hearing her sudden grunt of pain at the same time that she clutched his shoulder. Tears were springing to her eyes, but she murmured a grateful "Thanks" in his ear. He swung her over the side of the wagon, with the eager help of some of the other men inside, and watched her settle slowly into the space vacated by the man with the vest. She closed her eyes with what Slocum thought was intense relief.

The good Samaritan, meanwhile, was struggling to get his foot into the stirrup and then pull himself up into the empty saddle. The horse resented the extra weight and stepped out a bit, the man looking frightened as he clung to the pommel with both hands. Pio managed to settle the horse down and get hold of the reins, which he passed into the man's hand.

"Think you can handle him?' Pio asked.

The man allowed himself a little smile that made Slocum like him better. "We'll soon see," he said.

"Those fellows have stopped up there on the ridge," said the salesman.

Slocum looked up to see Marcus Boyer's men watching them, standing their horses about half a mile away. "Notice they're not close enough so's you could recognize them," Slocum said. "They'll probably just trail us into town and not cause you any trouble."

There was a bit of whispering among the people in the wagon and then a boy sitting on his mother's lap said breathlessly, "What will you do then?"

Slocum smiled at the boy, starting to speak.

"Won't you go to the police?" someone else asked.

That startled Slocum, though he tried not to let it show. He thought about the two men he'd wounded or killed during the dawn escape, worried that the judge would already have filed a complaint and made sure that it was telephoned to the surrounding city police agencies as well as the Los Angeles County sheriff.

"That's exactly what we'll do," he said aloud. We'll go directly to the police."

Pio and Louise both gave him dark looks of warning which Slocum tried to counter with a tiny shake of his head, as if it were a spasm.

"Then if it's all settled," said the salesman, with a touch of irritation, "perhaps you folks would like to hear some more about Sunset Estates?"

"Of course!" said one of the dudes, and as the salesman resumed talking he slowly realized that their excitement was extending itself to cover the idea of owning land in this wonderful Wild West, where the bandits still chased honest folk through the desert on horseback. It was true that some of the men had a hard time taking their eyes off Louise, and some of the women were giving her cold and haughty looks, but most of the prospects were asking questions now, and the salesman couldn't miss the brightness in their eyes. By the time they were rolling back toward Pasadena he was sure he'd have at least ten thousand dollars in down payments from this one wagon alone.

When the wagon reached the outskirts of town the salesman decided to show his gratitude to his three guests with an extra favor. "Dixon," he said to the teamster beside him, "why don't we be takin' these folks right to the police station on the way through town?"

"I'm afraid we can't let you do that," Slocum said.

"Think nothing of it," said the salesman. "The station house is just a block or two out of our way."

There was a chorus of agreement from the other people in the wagon, everyone wanting to help the strangers out of their predicament, and now Slocum had some very different feelings. He was ashamed for the urge to have some sport with these folks, who were basically kind-hearted. And he knew he'd been stupid to tell them part of the truth.

"We appreciate your intentions," he said, "but I meant exactly what I said. We *can't* go to the police."

The salesman's eyes were suddenly as hard as the steel-grey curls of his hair. "And why not, might I ask?"

Slocum spoke a little more harshly than he meant to. "Because the law isn't always on the right side in a fight like this."

Now there were hard looks from the people in the wagon, and a few frightened ones as well. "What about the men out there?" the salesman demanded. "Are you tellin' us *they're* the law?"

Slocum glanced back at the four riders, who'd been forced to move in closer but were still hanging back by more than a block.

"Have you ever seen lawmen act so shy?" Slocum said.

"Can't say that I have," the salesman said doubtfully. "But that still don't tell me what's been goin' on."

"It's like I said before, someone's trying to steal this fellow's ranch—his and his mother's—but he's doing it in a way that looks legal from the outside." Slocum met the stares he was receiving, but he was still afraid that someone in the crowd would alert the authorities as soon as they were gone. "We've got some hard evidence that shows the thief for what he really is," Slocum told them, "and those men are trying to make sure we don't bring it into court. But none of this is likely to get sorted out in time if the police get into the picture."

The salesman was looking thoughtful, as if willing to believe, but the others in the wagon seemed a lot more skeptical. Slocum was watching their faces as they lurched along in the wagon and realized that most of the customers had come from settled towns and cities back East where the difference between right and wrong was a lot simpler. He knew he was losing their sympathy, and he cursed himself for his big mouth.

"He's telling you the truth," Louise said suddenly. She paused a moment, until she had everyone's attention, then lowered her eyes in a tragic manner. "I'm the one they're trying to protect. I'm a witness to the scheme, and if it weren't for these two men"—her voice broke a little, Slocum clenching his teeth to keep from grinning—"Well if it weren't for these fine men I don't think I'd be around to tell the story."

The mood changed immediately, as Louise had known it would. Even the other women in the wagon looked sympathetic or determined to keep her out of evil hands. Someone said, "Don't worry, honey, you're safe with us," and someone else said, "Amen!" Now it was the salesman who looked skeptical, glancing from the woman to Slocum and back again, as if the story had gotten a little too thick. But he only needed one look at his customers to know what they expected of him. "Dixon," he said. "I guess we'll be going directly to the office."

"We're obliged to you," Pio said.

The salesman looked at the boy, and something about his quiet sincerity seemed to make him feel better. "It's little enough that we do," he said. "Would there be any other help you'd be needing?"

"If your office is equipped with a telephone..." Pio began hopefully.

"And maybe a back door?" Slocum put in.

The salesman looked from one man to the other and nodded. "We got both," he said, "an' you're welcome to 'em."

19

The salesman's office was in a brand new brick building, part of a full block of new buildings on Raymond Avenue not far north of Colorado. There was a trough in front for the wagon team. Slocum and Pio watered the three grullas there, then stripped their saddles and blankets and watched the animals roll in the dusty street. The men let their eyes drift up to the riders looking on from the edge of town. Now there were only three.

"The judge is gonna know pretty soon," Slocum said bitterly. "In a few more hours he'll have twenty men between here and Los Angeles, waiting to stop us from going in."

"It's a big city," Pio said. "They can't watch everyone."

"Yeah, but he knows exactly where we're going."

"The courthouse, you mean."

Slocum nodded.

"If we're not already too late," Pio said moodily.

They weren't. The salesman showed Slocum how to use the telephone on the wall and then went back to his customers, handing out cool water from an icebox as well as coffee and small finger cakes, answering questions about roads, utilities, interest rates, and penalty assessments while Slocum shouted into the horn. Eventually he was connected to the clerk of courts, and a minute later he hung up the earpiece.

"Ten o'clock tomorrow morning," he told Pio and Louise. "Courtroom number two."

"Thank heaven!" said Louise.

The salesman left one of his customers bending over a chalky blue plat map and approached the trio, looking intently from face to face. "Would you folks kindly join me in the back room?" he said, passing them on the way toward the rear of the building. He stopped a few paces away, finding it necessary to urge them with a swing of his head. "Come on," he said with a twinkle in his eye. "There're no monsters back here."

They entered the room cautiously, alert when the salesman glanced back once more and closed the door behind him. Finally he gave Slocum a shrewd look. "Was I hearin' you mention the Church and Jameson Bank just now?" he asked. "That's the court you were going on about, the bankruptcy hearing?" Slocum nodded guardedly, and the salesman studied him a moment longer before turning to Pio. "Then you must be the Jameson boy. Am I right?" When Pio hesitated, the salesman grinned. "When it comes to land, lad, there ain't too many secrets these days. And when it comes to gettin' screwed by Marcus Boyer—pardon me, miss—you have a lot of company. If it's the Honorable Judge Boyer you're after, then I'm William Walsh and I'm at your service."

He shook hands all around, quickly explaining that he was a third partner in the subdivision he was trying to sell. "Some of us took a chance," he said with a shrug, "bought the land early, hoping maybe to make a dollar." The competition for hot prospects was fierce, but there was also a grapevine among the speculators, who had common interests. "This Boyer fella has been throwing a lot of weight around, an' not lookin' much where he throws it. One or two men I know he's already put out of business." A scowl clouded the man's features. "I ain't crossed him yet, but I'm thinkin' the man needs a lesson. Now, look, I'm neglecting my customers. Let me see if I can get a signature on a contract or two, an' then we'll be talkin'. Will you wait?"

The three exchanged glances. "Mind if we wait out front?" Slocum said.

"Where you can keep an eye on me?" Walsh said with a grin. "Of course, man, and it's a credit to you. You have no reason in the world to be trustin' me. Not yet, anyway."

Slocum enjoyed watching the man work with his gift for talk, reassuring the hesitant, bolstering the confident. He told women of the cultural opportunities and men of the robust business and agricultural boom. He talked about the health benefits of living in the desert, and rhapsodized on southern California's weather. "But I have to warn you," he would say with a frown, waiting for the sudden look of worry on the customer's face, "it's only fair to tell you that we have a couple of months when there might be a little rain." There was a surge of relief when the customer found that this possible stumbling block to the decision he was just about to make was in fact no stumbling block at all. In a couple of cases, the customer was signing a mortgage within the next minute, and a bank draft the minute after that. Walsh collected the drafts, made some marks on his plat maps, and saw his last customer to the door about an hour after they'd returned from the desert.

"Now let me check on something for you," Walsh said when he closed the door. "I had an idea." He went to the telephone and cranked the handle. When he asked for the Pasadena police station Slocum got up and drifted over to his side, just in case. Walsh asked for a specific name, then put his hand over the mouthpiece while he explained that he had a friend on the force. "The Irish have to stick together," he said with a wink. The salesman asked his friend if there were warrants out on Louise Spring or John Slocum, waited for three or four minutes, then hung up. "It appears the police aren't on *any* side," he said. "So far."

"Maybe the judge doesn't want to take chances on the stories we could tell," Slocum said thoughtfully. "Someone might start investigating."

"You didn't ask about me," Pio said.

"Aye, for the name is well known hereabouts. I wanted to plant no ideas."

"Do you have ideas of your own?" Slocum asked.

"Only that you arrive safely in court, lad." He shook his head and laughed. "I wish I could be there to see it. But I know the next best thing." He cranked the telephone again and asked for the Los Angeles *Times* city desk, suggesting to an editor—if it wasn't already planned—that it might be profitable to have a man at the bankruptcy hearing in courtroom two at ten o'clock the next morning. Walsh winked at Slocum and said into the telephone that it was an anonymous tip.

"A wonderful invention," Slocum marvelled when Walsh had hung up. "What won't they think of next?"

"I wish we could crawl through the wires to get inside the courthouse," Louise said.

The three men smiled, and then Walsh was eyeing their clothes. "You'll be wantin' to clean up," he told them. "And to rest, I'm thinkin'. My home is at your disposal."

Again the three looked at each other. "We'd make a lot better appearance in court," said Louise.

"That cinches it," Slocum told Walsh. "We'll take you up on that offer. But first we have to do something about the gentlemen waiting for us outside."

"And the horses," Pio said.

"As for them"—the salesman glanced out the window—"No reason I can't put them up when I take the wagon back to the livery barn."

"You'll see they're brushed down, and fed well?"

"Nothing but the best." Walsh had a merry laugh. "An' I wonder which one of those poor fellows outside will have to spend the night in the stable, keeping an eye on your stock."

The others laughed with him. "Might as well leave our bags on the horses," Slocum said. "That'll help to keep 'em guessing."

Pio was the first to turn serious. "Mr. Walsh," he said impulsively, "those animals outside are some of the best we have on the ranch. Pick your favorite. It's yours."

"Well, now," the salesman said gravely, "I don't know that my room rates are runnin' that dear." But he was watching Pio closely, and when he felt satisfied that the boy was sincere—that refusal would be an insult—he put a big hand on the boy's shoulder. "It's a generous gift, lad, and I thank you. Now let me tell you where to come. I'll be expectin' you any time tonight."

Bill Walsh held a finger to his lips and crept across a dark storeroom to the back door he'd promised them, unlocking it and easing it open for a quick look into the alley. When he stood aside, Slocum led Pio and Louise through the opening. They hesitated a moment, blinking in the dusky half-light between two rows of four-story buildings. The door clicked shut behind them.

"Hey!"

The yell came from the east end of the alley, followed by a whistle. All three turned in time to see a rider in the open street, nearly hidden by the corner of the last building, waving wildly to someone else—apparently the two remaining pursuers watching the front.

"Christ!" said Slocum. "Let's get the hell out of here!"

They began running away from the rider just as he spurred his horse into the alley, hunkering low in the saddle. The pounding of hooves reverberated down between the walls and Slocum unlooped the thong from the hammer of his Colt, slipping it into his hand still running flat out. He twisted around for a look behind him, but the rider was apparently holding his fire. Slocum figured it would have to be a one-in-a-hundred chance for the bastard to hit anything anyway. And probably both sides were reluctant to alert the police.

They had almost reached the mouth of the alley when the other two riders appeared there, coming at them on the run. Louise turned and began running the other way.

"No!" Slocum bellowed. "We have to get past them!"

The girl turned again, losing her momentum in the same instant that one of the riders was upon her. He leaned over and grabbed her around the waist, but he hadn't reckoned with Slocum being so close behind her. While he was still leaning over in the saddle, Slocum swung the barrel of his colt across the man's temple. The rider slid off into the dirt, a dead weight on top of the girl. She was struggling to get out from under him, but Slocum and Pio were busy with the other two gunmen. One of them aimed a loop of rope for Pio and pinned his arms. The third one, the one who had sounded the alarm, was on his way to running Slocum down with his horse. Slocum turned to face the rush as if too startled to move, but in the last second he dove off to the left away from the rider's gun hand. The man tried to slash at him with the weapon, but it was awkward, and in that instant he had run on by.

Slocum rolled over in time to see Pio being yanked forward at the end of a rope. But the boy was reaching down, fumbling beneath his pants cuff. There was a flash of steel as he jerked a knife from the top of his boots and swirled his body around. It looked like a kind of dance step, but Pio had raised his knife hand from the elbow, to chest level, just enough to slice the rope on a keenly honed blade.

In the next instant Pio had slipped the loop of rope over his head and was running toward the rider who had thrown it, the knife still in his hand. With his gun still in its holster, the rider spun his horse and spurred it toward the street, immediately ramming into the third rider, who had swung around for another try at Slocum. Both horses reared, screaming, and both men fell into the dirt.

In the confusion, Slocum got Louise to her feet and ordered Pio to follow him around the corner. They were in public view now, a sweaty, dirty, ragged bunch scrambling down the boardwalk, pursued by two more men who looked just like them. The stares they were getting made Slocum want to laugh.

"Wait a minute," he said suddenly. "Why the hell are we running?"

Pio shrugged as they trotted along. "We've evened the odds, haven't we?"

They trotted across a wide street, weaving between buggies and wagons. Then Slocum pointed toward the mouth of the next alley. "How about here, Pio?"

The boy shrugged again, a humorous light in his eyes. "Why not?" He took Louise by the arm and guided her into the alley, yanking her to a stop as soon as they'd made the turn. "Wait here," he said when she looked puzzled. He went back to join Slocum at the corner of the building. Both men were heaving, their mouths open wide to quiet their breathing. They heard the pounding of their pursuers' footsteps slow down near the alley. The judge's men were being cautious. When they didn't appear immediately Slocum and Pio looked at each other, shrugged in unison, and stepped around the corner.

The judge's men looked startled. One of them yelled. Slocum landed a fist in his belly, then brought his locked hands down on the man's neck when he doubled over. Pio landed a neat left–right on the other man's jaw. He sank to the ground next to his partner.

Slocum gripped Pio's arm, gasping for breath. "I think we make a fine team, son. Now let's see if we can't give these fellows the slip."

The real estate speculator had a surprise for them in the morning. "I've been wanting to see the great Marcus Boyer get his comeuppance," he said brightly, "an' I've decided that's exactly what I'll be doin' today. One of the other partners can handle the sales. I can drive you into town."

That solved a problem for Pio, Slocum, and Louise. With money from Slocum's pocket, Walsh hired a closed coach.

The Irishman told them later he was the subject of some thorough inspections from several hard-looking men on the way but he stared them down or refused to stop. The coach pulled up in front of the courthouse a few minutes before ten o'clock. Slocum and Pio stepped down first, then Louise got out to walk close between them. Five or six men, apparently loungers, began converging on the trio. They stopped when they saw that Pio and Slocum each clutched a cocked revolver in each fist. There were no incidents as the tight-knit trio made its way up the courthouse steps and through the door.

Once they were through the door, Pio and Slocum slipped their weapons into their belts beneath conveniently outsized coats provided by Walsh.

Courtroom two was on the second floor.

20

Maria Jameson was slumped listlessly behind the left-hand counsel's table in front of the still empty bench. Slocum was surprised to see the ponderous figure of Wade Franklin beside her. At the right-hand table was Judge Marcus Boyer, apparently acting in his own behalf, and sitting next to him was the erstwhile Deadwood stage guard Tom Pierce. It was a good guess that Pierce was filling Slocum's old shoes. In any case, he was the first to notice the trio's arrival, turning his sharp eyes to the back of the room as soon as he heard the doors open. Pierce whispered a word or two to the judge, who swung his bony head around on his skinny neck and glared with such hatred and anger that Slocum felt an uncomfortable chill in the pit of his stomach.

"Pio!" Maria shouted. She was up from the table, pushing through the gate that separated the arena from the spectators' section, and coming toward her son with a glad smile animating an otherwise haggard face. She embraced the boy, then held him at arm's length to look him over, her voice quietly dignified but no less intense. "I did not know if you were alive or dead!" she told him, then turned to embrace Louise and finally Slocum, treating him to a special look all his own. "You have done well," she said to them, her eyes beginning to shine with tears. "Even if we lose everything today, we have not lost each other."

Slocum saw Walsh taking a seat on the wooden benches in the rear, with a short nod in Slocum's direction. Then Franklin was coming up behind Maria Jameson, wearing a patient and worldly expression. "I don't know why you've bothered to come," he sighed. "I told you it would do no good."

"And I told you that you were discharged," Pio said bitterly. "Mother, what is *he* doing here?"

"I didn't know what else to do," Maria Jameson faltered. "The hearing was going on anyway, and I . . . he just sat down as though nothing . . ."

"Of course I did," Franklin said soothingly. "You can't face a thing like this without representation. Now, why don't we all sit down and—"

"If you know what's good for you," Pio said through tight lips, "you'll leave this courtroom."

"But this is preposterous—"

Pio took a stop forward and something in his eye made the lawyer shrink away. He glanced at the boy's mother and saw no help there. "Very well," Franklin said, suddenly angry. "If you're going to dismiss your attorney at a time like this, then I'm better off without such fools for clients." He stalked to the counsel's table and gathered up his papers, his face turning a bright shade of red, and left the courtroom without another word.

Slocum was noticing the way Boyer watched Franklin leave. As the doors closed behind him, the judge leaned toward Pierce and whispered something in his ear. Pierce nodded and rose from the table, passing down the aisle as Slocum and Louise followed the Jamesons back toward the table where Maria had been sitting. Pierce brushed past Slocum without meeting his eyes, and Slocum turned to watch him go with a worried frown. He had a feeling he should be following the man, but he also knew he couldn't leave Maria and Pio Jameson alone during the hearing.

Slocum glanced at the clock over the rear door as he sat down. It was now one minute after ten. He looked toward the bailiff beside the high wooden bench, who had apparently just satisfied himself that both sides were as ready as they were going to get. The bailiff stepped back to open a door behind the bench, said a few words through the space, then threw the door open wide and stood at attention.

"All rise," said the bailiff. "This court is now in session, the Honorable Gregory Rolland presiding."

Slocum studied the tall, white-haired man in the black robe who stepped up behind the bench. The judge had a round face with a small rounded mouth and round grey eyes that gave nothing away. Slocum could imagine intelligence behind those eyes, maybe even a capacity for humor, but it might only have been wishful thinking. The judge certainly wasn't smiling while the bailiff announced the case. He arranged some papers in front of him, then glanced up to each side and finally rested his elbows on the bench, his folded hands beneath his chin in a pose that was to become familiar.

"Are you really representing yourself, Marcus?" asked the judge.

"See?" Pio hissed in Slocum's ear. "Just like old friends. What chance do we have?"

Slocum silenced the boy with a scowl.

"I expect this to be a simple and routine matter," Boyer told the judge. "I think the documents speak for themselves."

Judge Rolland leaned across his bench, frowning down at the papers before him, then looking at the other table. "Says here that Wade Franklin is appearing for the defendant," he said. "Where is brother Franklin?"

"We've dismissed him," said Pio.

Slocum leaned closer and whispered, "Stand up when you address the judge. And use his title."

"Dismissed him?" Rolland repeated.

Pio got to his feet. "That's right, Judge. We felt that he didn't have our best interests at heart."

"Do you have other counsel?" asked the judge. Slocum thought he saw a look of genuine concern, a desire for a fair hearing.

"Not exactly," Pio stammered.

Rolland stared at the boy, his eyes softening by degrees.

"Are you," he said suggestively, "requesting a continuation until you can find another attorney?"

That was enough for Slocum to take a gamble. He stood beside Pio and said, "Your Honor, is it required that each side be represented by a member of the bar?"

"It's certainly well advised, sir."

"Unfortunately, in this case, there has been some difficulty in finding another lawyer." The judge looked perplexed, but Slocum continued smoothly as Pio sat down. "Judge Boyer is correct, however, when he says the case is a simple one. There is no question that he loaned the Church and Jameson Bank a sum of money in return for mortgages. It is also a matter of record that Maria Jameson"—a nod at the black-haired woman sitting on the other side of Pio—"signed such a mortgage. And it's public knowledge that the bank in question was forced to close its doors the day before yesterday."

Judge Rolland was looking very stern. "Sir, I must warn you—"

"But there is one other factor to be considered," Slocum persisted, hesitating slightly, "although I confess I'm not sure how to go about introducing it."

"You can try plain language," the judge said. "It's my job to tell you whether it's a valid point of law."

"Thank you, Your Honor." Slocum frowned again, apparently unsure of himself, then blurted out his question. "Can Marcus Boyer profit from this transaction if it's proven that he committed fraud?"

Boyer was immediately on his feet, shouting for attention above the sudden rush of excited whispers in the courtroom. Slocum turned toward the rear, trying to hide his triumphant smile, and noticed a man in a grey suit scribbling in a notebook. Walsh gave Slocum a wink. When he turned back, the judge was scowling at the spectators. They quieted down within seconds.

"I think you'd both better approach the bench," Rolland said severely.

When they were standing side by side, Slocum could see that Boyer was trying hard to control himself, refusing to look his way. "This circus has gone far enough," he sputtered to Judge Rolland. "I will not tolerate it."

The white-haired man stared down at Boyer for a long moment, his chin once again propped on folded knuckles. "You seem to forget that this is my court," he said mildly.

Boyer was looking roughly where the judge's elbows were, a muscle or a vein pulsing beneath his ear. "Yes, sir," he said.

"And you," Rolland said suddenly to Slocum. "What's your name, anyway?"

"John Slocum, your honor."

"For the record," the judge said to the court reporter, "John Slocum is representing the defendants in this action. We're now going off the record."

The reporter leaned back and folded his arms. Rolland turned his full force on Slocum, a presence that made itself felt even though the judge was speaking in a barely audible murmur. "Mr. Slocum, do you realize you've made yourself vulnerable to a slander judgement if you can't back up what you said just now in open court?"

"With your permission, Your Honor, we have a witness here who can do just that. I was hoping we could call her as a witness."

Rolland looked over Slocum's head. "Are you referring to the young woman seated with the Jamesons?"

"Yes, sir. Her name is Louise Spring."

"A common whore!" Boyer hissed. She has nothing at all relevant to this proceeding."

"You know who she is, then?" whispered the judge.

"Only in a general way," Boyer stammered. "I've made it a point to . . . to keep informed on all aspects of this case."

The white-haired judge stroked his chin thoughtfully for a moment, then turned to Slocum. "Maybe you'd better tell me what her testimony would be, sir."

"You mean just tell you what she'd say?"

Rolland smiled. "It's all right," he said. "In jurisprudence it's called an offer of proof."

Slocum went through the whole story, from Mark Weber's orders to his own rescue efforts. Boyer shifted his feet and fumed silently by his side. As the implications became obvious, the judge let his penetrating eyes drift toward the sickly little man and stay there. There was a brief silence after Slocum finished. Boyer was still shifting his feet beneath Rolland's gaze.

"An interesting story," the judge finally said, "but of course it's not a direct accusation against Mr. Boyer."

"Exactly!" Boyer snapped.

"I don't know who else would have benefited," Slocum said.

Rolland sighed. "That's merely speculation, Mr. Slocum. Nothing that can be considered in a court of law."

Slocum had the feeling he was being subtly coached. "But with that testimony, isn't there some way we could get Mark Weber in here to testify? A court order or something?"

Rolland rubbed his jaw, a hint of humor shining in his eyes. "You mean something like a subpoena?"

"That's it," said Slocum. "We'd like to subpoena Mark Weber."

"Gregory," Boyer whined, "surely you're not planning to—"

"I'm planning to give everyone a fair shake," Rolland said. "I'd think you would want this cleared up as much as anyone."

"Of course, but—"

"Then let's get this character in here. Find out what he's got to say for himself. Bailiff!" The big deputy came up to the judge's elbow and Rolland told him to find two other deputies in the courthouse. "If there aren't any hanging around," he added, "I'll be amazed, but if there aren't, call the sheriff and have him send some over. Pick up this Weber fellow at the Rialto. Tell my clerk I want him to draw up the subpoena."

Slocum chanced a look at Boyer. The little man's cheeks were pale and hollow, but he didn't look as frightened as Slocum thought he should. Slocum remembered the whispered conference with Tom Pierce and the latter's abrupt departure. He was the one who was beginning to worry. He was wondering what other steps he might have taken to protect the Jamesons.

"Your Honor," Slocum said tentatively, "could we go ahead and take Miss Spring's testimony while we're waiting? Kind of to lay the groundwork for calling Weber to the stand?"

"I'll object to that," Boyer murmured. "We don't know if this is really going anywhere."

Rolland considered a moment and said, "We might as well get it on the record, one way or another. If the girl's telling the truth, then *someone* is sure monkeying around with the law."

"I'm taking exception, then."

"Agreed," snapped the judge. "The reporter will note the objection and my ruling, and the protest."

Boyer sullenly turned on his heel and went back to his table. That left Slocum standing by himself at the bench, wondering if Boyer wasn't giving up far too easily. The judge looked down at him and almost smiled. "That means you can put on your witness."

"Thank you, Your Honor. And thank you for your patience."

Slocum returned to his seat with a serious loss of confidence. He had hoped that his wide experience in courtrooms would at least keep him afloat, even if none of the experience had been on the right side of the law. Now he was feeling increasingly overwhelmed by the routines and procedures that others took for granted, and of which he had only a minimal grasp. He was also understanding the necessity of thinking on his feet, his head reeling with a dozen questions. Where had Pierce gone? Why was Boyer giving up so easily? Could he be setting a trap Slocum didn't understand?

"Mr. Slocum?" prompted the judge.

"Excuse me, Your Honor. We would like to call Miss Louise Spring."

21

Louise had stated her name and been sworn in. Slocum thought she looked cool and collected, but it wasn't necessarily the girl he was worried about. He put his hand on Pio's arm and whispered, "This is going to be a rough time, son. Can you keep your damn mouth shut?"

The boy nodded and said, "I'll try."

Slocum squeezed his arm, stood up, and said, "Let's get the worst part out of the way right now, Miss Spring. Up until a couple of nights ago, is it true you were working as a whore?"

The girl looked startled just for a moment, then settled herself in the witness stand with a rigid, almost defiant expression. "A prostitute, yes. At the Rialto."

"You engaged in sex in return for money?"

"Yes."

Slocum saw that he had everyone's attention, and carefully began to take Louise through her story. She was twenty years old. She'd been working at the Rialto for a year and a half. Mark Weber had been the manager during all that time. Quite often he played the piano, a good way to keep an eye on the trade. He kept order in the brothel, but sometimes he got a little rough with the girls. About two months before—she wasn't sure of the date, but she knew it was some time in June—Weber had told her—

"Objection!" said Boyer. "This is clearly hearsay."

Slocum frowned. It made sense to him that one person shouldn't be able to testify about what someone else said. There were too many opportunities for mistakes in the translation. But now he had to figure out another approach. To his surprise, he found himself enjoying the challenge.

"Did you, recently, start doing anything different?" Slocum asked Louise. "Was there any change in your routine?"

"Well . . . just that I started spreading this rumor."

"What exactly were you doing?"

"Every time I had a customer," Louise said steadily, "I'd somehow get around to talking about money, and the bank scare."

"Then what?"

"Then I'd let on that the Church and Jameson Bank was in bad trouble, worse than the others. I'd make it sound like there was some kind of mismanagement there, and the bank wasn't likely to survive the scare."

"You told this to every customer?"

"Just about."

"And was it your own idea?"

"You mean to spread the rumor? Of course not! Why would I make up something like that?"

"Did someone else instigate your actions, then?" Slocum asked her.

"Instigate?"

"Was it someone else's idea?"

"Yes. It was Mark Weber's."

"I think I'll let it go at that," Slocum said. He wondered if he was really seeing a twinkle in the judge's eye.

"Mr. Boyer?" said Rolland.

The little man remained behind his table, giving Slocum a quick, venemous glance before beginning his cross-examination. Slocum thought the look said: "Watch this!"

"Miss Spring," Boyer said, "you testified that you told every customer about the troubles of the Church and Jameson Bank."

"I said almost."

"All right, then, *almost* every one. Just how many men would that be?"

Slocum put his hand over Pio's arm again. The tension

in the muscles made it feel like a branch from an oak tree.

"Could it be a thousand?" Boyer said when Louise hesitated. "Or eight hundred? Maybe only five hundred?" He leaned forward, his tone suddenly harsh. "How about it, Miss Spring? Could you have slept with five hundred men in the last two months?"

Slocum noticed the judge watching him with a puzzled frown.

"Uh . . . could I make an objection here?" Slocum asked.

"On what grounds?"

"Well . . . I don't see what the answer has to do with anything."

"If he's *trying* to say the question is irrelevant," Boyer said scornfully, "my answer is that I'm showing the witness's moral character."

"You're trying to impeach the witness on moral grounds?" said Rolland.

"Yes, Your Honor."

Rolland looked at Slocum again, waiting for further argument. It was obvious to Slocum that he was getting in over his head, but when he looked at Louise he knew there was a way out.

"If I can I want to withdraw the objection," he told the judge. "I think the witness can handle Judge Boyer's tactics, and maybe that's the best way for her to demonstrate her moral character."

"Very well," Rolland said reluctantly. "Proceed."

"Can you anser the question?" Boyer demanded.

"I don't know."

"Meaning you don't know how many men you went to bed with?"

"That's right," Louise said evenly.

"Anyone who could pay the price, is that it?"

"Yes."

"In other words, you would do anything for money."

"Well, not *anything*."

"No? By your own testimony you not only gave yourself

for money, but spread lies as well!"

"I didn't know that they were lies." Boyer's head came up with a start. "I mean, I didn't know one way or the other."

"But they could have been."

"Well . . . yes."

Boyer slowly got to his feet, leaning forward with his hands on the edge of the table. "Aren't you lying even now?"

"No."

"Aren't you being paid to lie under oath?" Boyer roared.

"No!"

"And we're supposed to believe that," Boyer said sarcastically. "You've been selling your body to men, hundreds of them, maybe thousands. You claim you told them lies, perhaps ruined a respected financial institution. But we're supposed to believe that *now* you're telling the truth? Is that it?"

Slocum felt Pio beginning to rise and clamped down on his arm. Louise was swaying, her chin trembling. Tears were running from her eyes.

"Which is it?" Boyer demanded. "Were you lying then, or are you only lying about it today?"

Boyer was still leaning over the table. Louise was trying to hold up under his stare and the staring eyes of everyone else in the courtroom. It was suddenly so quiet that they could hear the girl's short, unsteady breathing. Even so, they almost missed it when she whispered, "You could ask them."

"Ask who?" Boyer said.

"The customers. The men I told about the bank." Her voice was getting stronger, and Slocum was silently urging her on. "Don't take my word for it," Louise said. "They'll tell you I'm telling the truth." There was the hint of a smile on her lips. "I see a couple of them out there right now."

Slocum was grinning fiercely. He hadn't thought of that himself. He was aware of movement behind him as one man left the courtroom. *Let him go,* Slocum thought. *Prob-*

ably a family man. There'll be others.

Boyer looked at Louise for nearly a minute, then sat down. "One more question," he said. "Have you ever seen me before?"

"No."

"Or heard my name?"

"No."

Boyer suddenly shook his head and made a sound of disgust. "This is a farce, Your Honor. The girl's testimony is highly dubious on its very face, and in any case irrelevant to these proceedings. I move that it be stricken from the record, and I also would ask—I notice there is a reporter from the Los Angeles *Times* present—I hope the judge will direct that this testimony not be made public."

"I won't make any rulings just yet," Judge Rolland said slowly. "Mr. Slocum, do you have any other questions of the witness?"

"Can I do that, Your Honor?"

The judge had another close call with a smile. "It's called redirect."

Slocum stood up. "I guess I'd just like to ask, Miss Spring: Has anyone paid you to tell this story?"

"No," the girl said firmly. "As a matter of fact, it was my idea."

"Why did you testify?"

The bailiff eased through the door behind the judge and passed up a note.

"To make up for the damage I caused," Louise was saying. She looked at Pio and Maria Jameson. "I made a terrible mistake, letting myself be used like that. I hurt people. I'm trying to undo the hurt."

Judge Rolland had read the note. His eyes were suddenly unreadable again, his elbows on the bench, his chin resting on his folded hands. He stared first at Boyer then at Slocum, and the pit of Slocum's stomach was feeling colder than ever.

"I think that's all I wanted to ask," Slocum said.

The judge nodded to Louise. "You can step down, miss. Thank you for your testimony."

"Yes, sir," she murmured. "You're welcome." She, too, seemed to sense that something was wrong. But as she walked back to the table, she tried to meet Pio's eye. Slocum wasn't sure if Pio responded. From the corner of his eye he saw Maria put her arm around the girl. It made him feel better. At least that particular battle was half won.

The courtroom was turning silent again, all eyes on the judge. He still hadn't moved. Now he was staring off into a distant corner, apparently lost in thought. Finally he sighed.

"I'm going to adjourn this court indefinitely," Judge Rolland announced, "until I've had a chance to weigh the developments." There was a stir among the spectators. "I might as well tell you that Mark Weber has just been found shot to death. It would appear that he killed himself, leaving a confession that implicates another party entirely in this scheme."

The judge stood and the bailiff shouted "All rise" above the sudden burst of noise in the courtroom. Rolland paused for one more speculative look at Marcus Boyer before he disappeared through the door of his chambers.

Slocum sat down again in a daze. Boyer might yet pull it off, he thought, but it was more likely that they had won. The police would investigate. Judge Rolland was obviously skeptical. At the very worst the judge would let Maria Jameson sell off enough land to pay her share of Marcus Boyer's mortgage. Slocum's heart was swelling with the vision of life with the beautiful black-haired woman at his side.

Slocum turned to find Maria and Louise staring at him with puzzled expressions. Pio Jameson had disappeared.

"Where's the boy?" Slocum demanded.

Louise shrugged dejectedly and Slocum ran out of the courtroom looking for him. Pio wasn't in the hall or out on the street. The only familiar figures he saw were Marcus Boyer, about half a block away, and William Walsh, who was standing patiently by the closed coach at the foot of the courthouse steps. Slocum waved to the real-estate man and went back inside.

"I think Pio will get over it," Slocum told the women as he sat down again. "The important thing is that we've won."

"Have we?" said Maria.

"Of course! What did you think?"

"Isn't it hopeless, now, with no way to connect the rumor to Judge Boyer?"

"Not at all," Slocum said. "We've made enough of a fuss so that . . ." He broke off in mid-sentence, scaring the women with the look in his eyes. "Jesus Christ," Slocum said hoarsely. "I wonder if that's what Pio thought?"

"What's wrong?" demanded Maria.

"Stay here!"

Slocum was up and running, praying that he was wrong but afraid that he was right. If Pio Jameson also believed that the death of Mark Weber had closed off the last hope for saving their land, then Slocum had to get to Boyer before Pio did.

Slocum had to make sure the boy didn't kill the judge.

22

The next few minutes were a strange and unsettling time for John Slocum. For many years he would think back to them, trying to sort them out. He remembered pausing at the bottom of the courthouse steps to consider the coach in which he'd arrived. Walsh had opened the door, waiting for Slocum to enter, but the coach, which was black, looked too much like a hearse for Slocum's comfort. Possibly he was also influenced by the rational thought that the streets were too crowded, that it would be faster to run the few blocks between the courthouse and the Hotel Nadeau.

The open door of the coach, however, stayed in his mind as he ran through the busy sun-splashed streets of Los Angeles. His body flowed effortlessly along, arms and legs pumping, ladies in bright dresses stepping aside to let him through and staring at him as he passed. But the pounding of his boots on the boardwalk, the laughing shoppers, the carriages jangling by, all were strangely distant sounds in his ear. The modern stone buildings and brightly colored awnings above him, shading him from the brilliant sunshine, were strangely distant sights, as if they would disappear should he try to touch them.

His mind was dominated, even haunted, by the open door of the black coach and the black shadows inside. It almost seemed as if the street before him had been a giant painting and the door a passage through the canvas. He had the feeling that he was running toward that dark opening, and as he ran it filled with ghostlike images of Slocum's Stand in Calhoun County. Through the open doorway of the coach, in his mind's eye, he saw himself returning to the farm after the War, healing as slowly from the rifle bullet that collapsed his lung as the land healed from the scars of the war. He saw the judge and his hired gun warning him that they would take his land, and he saw himself oiling the Colt Navies. He wanted to cry out to the boy he had been, trying to warn him. Slocum ran wildly, but he never gained an inch on the vision in the doorway. The boy continued oiling the Navies, unable to hear the warnings of the man he would become.

Then the judge and the hired gun were driving down the road from town. Slocum the man, arms and legs flailing hopelessly as he ran, watched them come. The judge looked like Marcus Boyer at first, then turned into the fleshy and florid man he had truly been. They stepped down from the carriage, looking very sure of themselves. Slocum the boy came out to meet them while the man looked on in anguish, separated by twenty years. Slocum the man watched Colt Navies fly out of their holsters, watched the hired gun crumple to the ground before he could fire, watched the terrified judge stumble back with two bullets in his great belly. The judge died slowly, in agony, clawing in the dirt of Slocum's Stand. The boy had looked on, hardened by the stink of war, feeling nothing. But there was a terrible emptiness in Slocum's chest as he ran. That had been the end of one promising life and the beginning of another, not so promising, with twenty hard years between. He knew the rest of that story too well. He didn't want to watch it. He willed the images to fade. The open coach door faded slowly with them.

Slocum found himself in the lobby of the Hotel Nadeau. He hadn't seen Boyer or Pio anywhere. He was gambling that Boyer would simply return to his room because it was his only chance, the only place Slocum could think to look. It also might seen a safe haven for the man who, apparently, had just assigned his bodyguard to take care of the Rialto's piano player. Tom Pierce had not returned during the court session.

Slocum saw that the elevator was being used and decided to check the dining room, but the place was nearly empty and he established quickly that Marcus Boyer wasn't taking an early lunch. Slocum ran back into the lobby, scowling when he saw that the elevator was still on its way up. He cursed under his breath and raced for the stairs, climbing the landings that surrounded the caged shaft.

The counterweight whooshed down beside him, the lower cables still playing out. Slocum felt his heart pounding furiously and his legs turning liquid. He stumbled on the third floor, but kept running when he heard the elevator stop on the floor above him—Marcus Boyer's floor. He heard the clackety-clack of metal gates, a murmured word or two, and then again the clackety-clack. The elevator started down as Slocum left the landing between the two floors. He heard a creaking of floorboards just above, apart from Boyer's steps down the hallway.

Slocum reached the top steps in time to see Marcus Boyer unlocking the door to his suite, unaware of Pio Jameson padding up softly behind him. Slocum also saw the shine of steel held low in Pio's hand. He hollered something, still running. Boyer looked up with a startled expression. His hand snaked inside his coat, toward the pistol in the shoulder holster. Pio grabbed Boyer's wrist and pushed the little man back into his room, drawing his other arm back, so that the last thing Slocum saw as he ran was the boy's hand and the knife it held, before they disappeared.

Slocum lost heart, then, slowing for the last few steps. He almost collided with Pio as the boy backed out through the door.

Pio Jameson's hand and coat were splashed with blood. He was still holding the knife, but in his eyes was an expression of horror and revulsion. He looked blindly at Slocum, then stared through the doorway with his mouth working, making no sound.

"Well, well," Slocum said savagely, "you found out it ain't so pretty killing a man. Not hardly like gutting a steer, is it?" He wanted to beat the boy, but it looked like Pio was already eating at himself from the inside out, his eyes filling with tears as his mouth continued to work.

"Go on," Slocum told him. "Get the hell away from here as fast as you can. And if you ever . . . *ever* breathe a word about this to anyone, I'll whip you within an inch of your life." When Pio hesitated, Slocum grabbed his coat sleeve and shoved him violently. The boy stumbled, looking over his shoulder like a whipped dog, and Slocum whispered at him to get moving. "At least to the second floor, for now. Take off that damn coat and wrap it up. Hide the knife and get back to your mother."

"What will you do?" the boy stammered.

"Git!" Slocum yelled, taking a step forward.

When the boy was safely down the stairs Slocum stepped into the judge's suite, surprised to find Boyer still alive. The man was on his stomach, looking at his gun off in one corner, making feeble scratching motions on the floor as if he were trying to crawl. Slocum rolled him over with the toe of his boot. The judge stared up from sunken, fading eyes that could barely see. Slocum ripped away the coat, seeing where the knife had gone in at a mortal spot a few inches above Boyer's belt, opening the kidney and probably the spleen along with it.

As he stared at the blood oozing from the gash, Slocum brought his mind to focus for one clear instant that told him what he would do. In that instant he thought of his own life and the life Pio had before him. He weighed the love he shared with Maria Jameson and her love for Pio. He considered everything, from every angle, and there was only one answer. The decision was made in that same instant, never to be regretted. He pulled one of the Colts from beneath his coat and stepped back.

A spasm went through Marcus Boyer's body. Slocum didn't know if the man was still alive, reacting to what he saw was coming, or if it was the beginning of his death throes. Slocum had seen plenty of them, however, and he didn't much care.

"I can't say this is gonna bother me much," he whispered. In the distance he heard the elevator cranking up. Suddenly he filled his lungs and hollered as loud as he could. "You worthless skunk! I'll teach you to cheat a man!"

He aimed the Colt carefully and pulled the trigger three times. The concussion was a terrible thing in the closed room, but not nearly as terrible as the ripping and tearing of three .44 slugs through Boyer's flesh. Slocum grouped them over the narrow slit left by Pio's knife. He felt pretty sure there wasn't a coroner in the world who'd now be able to find the track of the blade.

Slocum was running again, gun still in hand. He went quickly down the hall, ignoring the horrified look of a woman geting off the elevator. He took the stairs two and three at a time, feeling an ache of weary sadness, but trying to look frantic and desperate instead.

He ran into the street, into the glaring sun, and heard a few shouts of "There he goes!" somewhere behind him. He was thankful when he didn't have to run more than four blocks. A policeman with a black mustache appeared suddenly from around a corner, levelling a revolver, ordering Slocum to halt.

Slocum skidded to a stop and raised his arms. "Yes, officer," he said meekly. He was handcuffed and led away.

He was looking forward to a little rest.

23

Slocum sat in a small, airless room on the first floor of the Los Angeles County jail, staring at a plasterboard wall painted grey. His expression was scornful and sometimes he allowed himself a sneering, evil smile. A police detective named Mike Forrette studied him for a long moment, brows furrowed in a puzzled frown. Finally the detective sighed.

"Let the record show that John Slocum is making this statement of his own free will," said Forrette, "having waived the presence of counsel." He paused, and the scratching of the police stenographer's pen filled the room. "Mr. Slocum, do you admit to murdering Judge Marcus Boyer at about eleven-thirty this morning?"

"Sure," Slocum said breezily. "I'd say there's enough witnesses around so there's no question about that."

"But some of those same witnesses, Mr. Slocum, saw a young man following the judge through town after the court hearing. They saw him lurking in the Hotel Nadeau. And the description they give of him—well, it fits young Pio Jameson to a T."

Slocum shrugged. "So?"

"So you never saw the boy yourself?"

Slocum shook his head.

"For the record, the prisoner indicates he did not," sighed the detective. "Are you sure that Pio Jameson had nothing to do with the shooting?"

"Look," said Slocum, "how many slugs did you find in the bastard's body?"

"Three, of course."

"And how many empty shells in my gun?"

"The point is—"

"Did you check Jameson's gun?" Slocum demanded. "Had it been fired?"

"Of course not, but—"

"Then forget it! I didn't see the boy, and even if I did I wouldn't want him taking any credit for what I done."

"Credit?"

"You heard me. The world owes me a favor for getting rid of Marcus Boyer. The man was no better than a cockroach."

"Yet you worked for him . . ."

"Sure," Slocum said defensively. "He paid good money. Or at least he did at first. It was his fault that I killed him."

"Am I to understand, then, that you shot him in a dispute over money?"

"Of course, man. What would you have done? I couldn't hardly go into court and say"—falling into a high, whining voice—"'Excuse me, but this man wouldn't pay me for helping him cheat and kill.' I had no choice."

"You say the dispute was over money," Forrette offered, "and yet you missed a perfect opportunity to reward yourself."

"What's that supposed to mean?"

"The judge's tin box, of course. The famous tin box. It was sitting in plain view on the bed."

Slocum tried to keep the hard look in his eyes while he cursed himself, and while the detective studied him with a shrewd look. "I just didn't see it, that's all. I was too busy trying to get away from a murder charge."

"There was more than a hundred thousand dollars in that box."

Slocum suddenly smiled. "I should have noticed," he said in a carefree way. "But I bet the fellows on the force are glad I didn't, right?"

"What?"

Slocum winked at him. "Come on, how much was *really*

in that box? You can tell me! The stenographer here won't write it down. How much went into the widows' and orphans' fund?"

Forette's face went blank with fury. He stood up, towering over Slocum, raising his hand to strike. Slocum steadied himself, but slowly the detective regained control and sat down again with a sidelong glance at the stenographer, who was busily scratching at his pad. The detective looked at some notes on his lap, and Slocum breathed a quiet sigh of relief.

"According to our investigation," the detective said, "you were merely a bodyguard for the judge, and that employment apparently ended a few days ago."

"That's the way he wanted it to look."

"Are you saying it's not true?"

"That was his was of getting someone out on the ranch to keep an eye on the woman and her kid. He knew they weren't going to take things lying down."

"He already had someone there, a Thomas Pierce."

"Yeah, one man for the whole ranch. The way I did it, I was in on everything those people were thinking. I also managed to get the whore out of town, so she wouldn't get any ideas about going to the authorities over the bank deal."

"Just how did you manage all of this, Mr. Slocum?"

"We staged a murder attempt on me the night I killed old Will Church. Then I went to the whore with a story about her life being in danger, and with the help of Mark Weber she got to believin' it." Slocum laughed and slapped his knee. "She sure was scared," he said, and went on to tell the rest of the story, up until the morning of his escape from the ranch.

"One man was killed and another wounded in that action," Forrette interrupted. "Was that also part of the scheme?"

"I wasn't sure they was in on it," Slocum said harshly. "Besides, what's another killing where the judge is concerned? He sure was shrewd, that one."

The detective looked disturbed, staring at Slocum with obvious distaste. "Your claim, then, is that Judge Marcus Boyer was masterminding a series of events that would lead to his acquisition of the Church and Jameson ranches?"

"Exactly! That man wasn't gonna leave nothing to chance. He had Weber telling the whore—"

"Her name is Miss Louise Spring."

"Sure. Weber had the . . . had Miss Spring spreading the rumor to everyone she could, just to make sure the bank would fail. Weber didn't like it too well, but the judge had me pay him a visit." Slocum rubbed his hands and laughed. "After that he was very cooperative."

"The records show that Boyer had a controlling interest in the Rialto."

Slocum shrugged, keeping the surprise from his face. "There you are," he said, as if that proved everything.

"So you have direct knowledge that the judge was responsible for those rumors being spread?"

"I just told you."

The detective scratched his head. "Weber's statement says it was Will Church, that the man was trying to get control of the bank for himself."

"That's crazy," said Slocum. "The one thing I'll tell you straight is, that old man wanted to die. He made me shoot him down. I saw it in his eyes."

Mike Forrette looked at his notes. "That's pretty much corroborated by the witnesses," he said. "But how do you explain Weber's statement?"

"I'd say Boyer put him up to it, just to be safe. That little man was getting pretty desperate." Slocum snapped his fingers. "Say, does that statement actually say anything about suicide?"

The detective frowned thoughtfully. "I guess not."

"There you go. The judge had him write it, Weber thinkin' he's supposed to leave it behind when he makes a run for it. Then someone walks up behind him and . . . pow!" Slocum pointed a finger, pulled an imaginary trigger.

Forrette was nodding thoughtfully. "It could be," he said, allowing himself a quick smile at Slocum. "Too bad you're not wearin' the uniform, Slocum. You'd'a made a dandy detective."

Slocum laughed with a bitterness Forrette didn't understand. The detective looked a little sad as he sorted through his notes. Suddenly he looked up, a curious expression on is face. "Funny how life works, isn't it, though? You got an early start in your career of killing judges."

This time Slocum showed his surprise. "How the hell did you know about that?" he demanded.

"Your former employer's tin box, again. He had a couple of old Wanted posters on you, maybe thinkin' to hold you in line if it became necessary. We sent a couple of wires to check them out. Killed your first man—outside the law, anyway—a few months after the War. Twenty-odd years ago. As it turns out he was a judge, too."

Slocum stared at the grey wall for a long time, the detective waiting patiently for a comment. In the end the detective leaned forward to catch Slocum's soft words.

"Yeah," Slocum said, "life sure is a bundle of tricks, ain't it?"

Two hours later Slocum was telling more or less the same story to a very eager reporter from the Los Angeles *Times*, the same man he had seen in Judge Rolland's courtroom. Slocum tried to play down his role of double agent on the Rancho Cabrillo, but apparently the reporter had already seen a transcript of the confession.

"It looks, by the way, like the judge's rumor was made up out of whole cloth," the reporter told Slocum near the end of the interview. "The government began an audit of the Church and Jameson Bank after the doors closed. Nothing official yet, but I'm hearing hints that everything was in fine order."

"Maybe the bank isn't dead, then?"

"I've never heard of such a resurrection," the reporter

said with a frown. "They closed without a penny left. How could they start up again?"

John Slocum was splashed across the front page of the *Times* the next morning, a Saturday. There were separate stories on the court hearing, Mark Weber's death, Judge Boyer's murder, and Slocum's remarkable jailhouse confession. The reporter had played up what he called Slocum's penchant for killing judges.

Tuesday's newspaper contained the answer to the reporter's question on resurrections. Maria Jameson had announced early on Monday that she was reopening the bank with an unspecified amount of money—Slocum knew it was Will Church's insurance settlement of forty-five thousand dollars—and that she hoped the depositors would give the institution a second chance. Her primary goal, however, was to see that no one suffered from the bank's failure.

The same paper carried a story saying that government auditors had found the bank to be well managed, with no evidence of misappropriations.

A third story said that Judge Gregory Rolland had ordered Marcus Boyer's estate to relinquish any claim on a loan to the bank, and any outstanding mortgages connected with that transaction.

Slocum smiled as he read.

On Tuesday afternoon, the jailer announced that Maria Jameson was waiting to see him.

24

Slocum wasn't prepared for the emptiness he felt when he saw her. Maria Jameson had already been turning into a memory during Slocum's long hours in the cell, hours during which he'd gone over everything that had happened at least a hundred times. With all that time to think he had turned everything around and looked at each step he took, and the answer always came out the same: there was nothing he would have done differently—that is, of course, if you didn't count keeping a closer eye on Pio Jameson. But once Pio was gone it seemed that Slocum's course was set. And everything that he had done had worked out just the way he wanted it to. Pretty soon he was telling himself that one woman more or less didn't matter; he was really still too young to settle down anyway. He started looking forward to eventual freedom and more adventures.

But that all changed when Maria Jameson walked into the meeting room.

Her dark eyes were full of sorrow as she tried to make a joke. "If they're watching," she said with a weak smile, "they'll wonder that I'm not trying to thrash you for the traitor that you are."

Slocum looked puzzled for only a moment. "Oh, you mean the newspaper stories. Perhaps you should try, just for show."

Suddenly she shuddered. "If only I could hold you!"

"The fact you can't is worse than any thrashing, Maria." He studied her face. "Do you know, then?"

She nodded. "Pio wouldn't tell at first, but I knew anyway, because I knew what was in his heart when he left the courtroom. Just as I know what is in yours. Those stories were frightening, I confess—for a second or two. But as I read them I began to see your design—and your love."

The woman closed her eyes and tears appeared in the corners, flowing freely down her cheeks. Slocum lifted a hand without thinking, and let it fall uselessly in his lap with a clanking of the irons on his wrist.

"If only they could know what I know," Maria said. She opened her eyes and held them steady. "If only they could see you for the rare breed of a man you are, and understand how great is my loss."

"*Our* loss," said Slocum. "My resolution weakened when I thought of leaving you behind forever."

She threw up a small white hand. "No! Don't say forever! I could never bear to let you rot in this . . . I'll find some way to free you."

Slocum smiled for the first time. "That's one thing that's already taken care of, Maria. I never planned to serve a sentence." The haunted look returned to his eyes. "But it also doesn't mean I'll be able to stick around."

"Times change, though, and people forget. You will not always look the same. I must have hope that someday . . . Please, dear God, don't say forever."

"Sure," said Slocum.

They gazed silently at each other for perhaps two minutes, wanting to talk for a lifetime. In the distance there was the sound of a cell door slamming.

"Is the bank still open?" Slocum finally asked.

"Oh!" Maria was smiling, a spark of life in her eyes. "There are lines around the block again, but they're putting money *in.* Some of them are even apologizing to the tellers for taking their money out in the first place. It's wonderful! The city has rallied to our cause."

"I'm glad," said Slocum.

Another minute went by, and somewhere another cell door closed.

"Louise has gone away," Maria said.

"I'm sorry to—"

"But I think she'll be back in a few months, when Pio has had a chance to forget. And to miss her."

"Do I sense a bit of woman-to-woman advice?"

Maria smiled.

"My father always said it was a conspiracy," Slocum told her. "The mothers and other women against their sons."

"He wants to confess, you know. It has hurt his pride that I wouldn't let him," Maria said.

"Did you explain?"

"I tried. He goes away and thinks about it."

"He'll work it out. He's got a twenty-year head start."

Slocum regretted the words, afraid they sounded like self-congratulation, but Maria only looked at him. More time passed, and neither one could find more words. Slocum thought it was a strange thing. He would have thought there'd be a million things for them to say to each other. And maybe there were, and because of that there was also nothing to say. It was a question of: Where do you start? In the end you realized it was pointless to start anywhere.

Maria sighed, shifting in her chair. She leaned forward and kept her voice low. "The paper says there will be a trial."

Slocum nodded. "Already set, for Thursday."

"But I don't understand. If you already signed a confession . . ."

"The courts always go through the motions when it comes to first-degree murder. I guess they want to make twice as sure before they hang you."

Maria looked horrified. "You said I didn't have to worry."

Slocum grinned reassuringly. "You'll see. I've kept an ace up my sleeve."

"Is it something about the trial?"

"Not exactly."

"But you really do have a way out?"

"Absolutely. Don't worry for even a moment."

She gave him a sad smile. "That's so easy for you to say." She gazed at him another minute, the smile slowly fading and leaving only the sadness. "Well," she said after a while. She wore a puzzled frown, as if she, too, wondered why there wasn't more to say. "I guess I'll go, John."

Slocum felt his heart breaking. "I'm glad you came," he said simply.

The woman nodded, still frowning, tears again forming in her eyes. "Until the day you return, then . . ."

"Sure, Maria."

25

"Did you really ask to see me, Mr. Slocum?"

It was Wade Franklin, the former Jameson attorney, standing uncertainly before Slocum's cell. His bulk was enough to spread across four bars.

"None other," Slocum said cheerfully. "After all, I have a murder trial coming up in a couple of days."

"Well, now." The lawyer cleared his throat. "I've read the newspapers, Mr. Slocum, and frankly I'm not sure I'd be interested in taking the case."

Slocum bounded off his cot and stood face to face with the sweating attorney. *"I'm* not particularly interested in going to trial, Franklin. That's the real reason you're here."

"I don't understand you."

Slocum thrust his face through the bars. "Think back to a certain visit to your office, Franklin. More important, think back to a few minutes after those three people left. More important still, do you recollect a certain telephone conversation with the deceased Judge Boyer?"

"Oh, Christ!" said Franklin.

"'Slocum is the one to worry about,'" Slocum mimicked. "'I think we can look forward to a long and prosperous association.'"

"Oh, God. How did you—"

"An open window, Franklin. I smelled your stink from a mile away, so we went around to listen. It's the one thing I haven't mentioned to the constables. Yet."

"You can't prove anything," the lawyer said desperately.

"There were three of us listening, you scum. The Jamesons know you sold them out. But don't forget the operator's testimony. Or the records where you do your banking. Have you deposited the judge's money yet?"

"Oh, Christ."

"Exactly. But you have a chance, Franklin."

"A chance?"

"To repent and try again, maybe even to serve justice."

"By representing you?"

"By making sure you don't *have* to represent me. If I go to trial, then I'll be forced to tell everything I know."

Franklin's loose, heavy body sagged in front of the bars. "What do you want, Slocum?"

"Not much. A small pistol, a little traveling money, and a sleeping car on the Union Pacific. In anyone's name but mine."

"When?"

"Thursday."

"The first day of the trial?"

"I want to see you make your opening statement, Counselor."

"Oh, God."

"Besides, it'll be easier to make a run for it out in the open. And with all the public contact, no one will ever suspect it was you who gave me the pistol."

"Thanks for your concern," Franklin said in a dry tone.

"I should see that you're disbarred, damn it!"

The attorney hung his head. "It was a terrible thing to do," he said, "but I was broke, and—"

"Save it, Franklin."

"Really, though. I'm not that sort. It won't happen again."

"There's probably a chance in a million you're telling it straight." The lawyer looked as if he was about to cry. "Aw, shit," said Slocum. "Just go home and write a good opening argument. Use your imagination."

"I came to tell you I understand."

This was Pio Jameson, conducted to the meeting room

by detective Mike Forrette himself. The detective gave the two men a peculiar look before he closed the door behind him.

"I think he knows," Pio whispered.

"He doesn't 'know' anything, son. He just senses it. His nose is twitching because the pieces don't quite fit. But there isn't a thing in the world he can do about it." Slocum smiled. "That's part of what bothers him."

Pio stared at the floor. "Well, anyway. It sounds silly to say thanks for giving me a second life. Your sacrifice is a noble thing, Mr. Slocum."

"Noble, hell," Slocum said. "It was just the obvious thing to do. Sacrifice? Shit, all I'm gonna do is go back to living the kind of life I was used to anyway. And, if you want to know, feelin' pretty good you won't be joining me. It seems like *just once* I oughta be able to pass along some of the benefit of what I've figured out."

"I believe you have, Mr. Slocum. I'll try to use well this life you've given me. I'll make something of myself for you to be proud of."

Slocum's eyes were suddenly shining. He blinked a couple of times and cleared his throat and said, "You already have, son. And your visit has made everything worthwhile, twice over."

26

By midnight on Thursday Slocum was dozing off somewhere north of Santa Barbara, comfortably stretched out in a Union Pacific sleeping car. A dreamy smile on his face meant he was remembering Wade Franklin's opening statement to the jury—a heartfelt discourse on justice and clemency for men who admit their mistakes.

The smile faded. He was remembering the presence of Maria Jameson in the courtroom, a presence that was almost unbearable for him. Pio was also there, and the smiling land salesman William Walsh.

Slocum frowned, eyes still closed under the bill of his pulled-down hat. Susan Bently was *not* there. Slocum had half expected to see her, to have a visit from her in jail. He began to hope that she had left the judge after the killing of Will Church.

He would never know. He never heard from her again.

Another missing person was Tom Pierce, whom Slocum last saw on his way out of the courtroom after a whispered talk with Marcus Boyer—and just before Mark Weber was found dead at the Rialto. Pierce was also never seen again.

Slocum smiled again, thinking about his financial condition. His fare was paid as far as Seattle. He had seventeen dollars in his pocket, the clothes he was wearing, and a three-dollar gun called the Swamp Angel, made by Forehand and Wadsworth.

That was the inventory of all his worldly possessions.

But there would be work in Seattle, perhaps up in one

of the lumber camps, and there would be plenty of poker games, and maybe there would be luck.

Good Lord, he was thinking, *things have to start running my way some time soon. I sure as hell am due after Los Angeles.*

Slocum started getting excited, finding it difficult to sleep, wondering how far he could go and how fast. He was thinking about new adventures, new women...

Then he was thinking about *the* woman. Her dark eyes and long black hair and fiery spirit floated vividly in his reverie. Sleep was finally overtaking him, and in his dreams he saw her still. He saw her at the end of the long road he was traveling.

He saw her waiting.